Yesterday's Dream

Judy Baer

Yesterday's Dream

Judy Baer

Guideposts®

CARMEL • NEW YORK 10512

In memory of
Grace Husie
and
Fred Swenson
whom I loved like
grandparents.

JUDY BAER received a B.A. in English and Education from Concordia College in Moorhead, Minnesota. She has had over fifteen novels published and is a member of the National Romance Writers of America, the Society of Children's Book Writers and the National Federation of Press Women.

Two of her novels, *Adrienne* and *Paige*, have been prizewinning bestsellers in the Bethany House SPRINGFLOWER SERIES (for girls 12–15). Both books have been awarded first place for juvenile fiction in the National Federation of Press Women's communications contest.

For God so loved the world that he gave his one and only Son, that whoever believes in him shall not perish but have eternal life.

John 3:16

Chapter One

"Lexi! Lexi, wake up."

Lexi Leighton moaned softly and pulled a pillow over her head. "No," she moaned. "It's too early. My alarm didn't go off yet." She burrowed her nose into the mattress and clamped her hands over her head. "I'll get up soon. Let me sleep a little longer."

"Lexi. You have to wake up now." Her mother's voice was anxious.

She glanced toward the window. The first rays of morning light had not even begun to peek over the horizon. It was dark as midnight outside. Lexi pulled the pillow away from her face and struggled to sit up. "What's wrong?"

The sight of both her parents, fully dressed and in their coats, startled Lexi. She swung her legs to the side of her bed and grabbed at her mother's arm. "Mother, what's going on?"

"Shhh," her mother said. "Don't be alarmed. Your father and I are going to drive to Grandpa and Grandma's house in Oxford City. Will you get Ben up in the morning and see that he gets ready for the Academy?" Though Lexi's mother was trying to appear composed, she was wringing her hands. Her eyes were red and puffy as though she'd been crying.

Lexi's father tapped his toe impatiently, something he never did unless he was nervous or upset. Lexi felt a spiral of fear burrow into her mid-section. "What's happened?" she demanded. She was no longer sleepy, but suddenly very frightened.

"We just got a call from Oxford City. Grandpa Carson has had a stroke."

A river of icy fear washed over Lexi leaving her cold and shivering. "Grandpa? Is he going to be all right?"

"We don't know anything more than what the social worker at the hospital said," Mrs. Leighton explained. "Grandma is with him. She wants us to come right away. I'm sorry we had to wake you. I know it will be hard for you to go back to sleep now. We have called the Goldens. Jennifer's parents wanted us to bring you and Ben over there immediately, but I thought Ben would sleep better in his own bed tonight. I know you are perfectly capable of taking care of him in the morning. The two of you can stay with the Goldens if we aren't back from Oxford City by tonight."

"Do you have any idea when you might be back?" Lexi wondered. Her heart was thudding like a big bass drum in her chest and her mouth felt dry and cottony.

Mr. and Mrs. Leighton exchanged worried looks. "No, Lexi, we don't know."

"Is . . . is Grandpa going to live?" Lexi stammered.

"We don't know that either, darling." Mr. Leighton laid a comforting hand on Lexi's shoulder. "We can't tell you anymore until we've been to the hospital. I know it will be hard, but try not to worry, and trust for the best."

"This is serious, isn't it, Dad?" A heaviness descended in Lexi's stomach. She felt as though she were going to be sick.

"Yes, honey, I'm afraid it is. Grandpa hasn't been in good health for many years. We're very worried about him."

"Well, don't worry about Ben and me," Lexi said. "We're going to be just fine. I'm not going to tell Ben how serious this is until we know some more facts. Grandpa will probably be better in a few days." She smiled at her parents, hoping she looked bright and confident instead of dark and frightened, like she felt.

"I *knew* we could count on you, honey." Mrs. Leighton gave her daughter a grateful hug. "You've made things much easier already. Thanks for being so understanding."

Lexi slipped on her slippers and robe to walk her parents to the front door. Mr. Leighton's car was already running. Lexi could see their bags in the back seat.

"Bye, honey. Be good. I'll call as soon as I can."

"Don't worry about me a bit. I'll be fine."

"Make sure Ben takes his sweater to school."

"He won't forget a thing, I promise."

"You know the number at Grandma's house. You can reach us if you need to."

"We won't need to."

Without another word, Mrs. Leighton threw her arms around her daughter and hugged her tightly.

Lexi could feel her mother's body trembling with emotion.

"Don't, Mom. Don't cry. Everything's going to be all right. I just know it is."

After Mr. Leighton had helped Lexi's mother into the car, he turned to speak to his daughter. "Thank you, Lexi."

"I wish there were something more I could do," Lexi said, feeling helpless.

"You've done enough. Not having to worry about Ben is a big relief for your mother." He paused. "There is one thing you can do, Lexi."

"Anything, Dad. What is it?"

"You can pray."

Lexi watched her father get into the car. She stared down the street after the vehicle until it disappeared around a corner, leaving her standing alone on the front porch of the house.

She shivered, not from the cool night air, but from fear.

Lexi walked into the house and locked the front door. She was wide awake now. It would be many hours before she could sleep. Her stomach was churning nervously. She padded to the kitchen, opened the refrigerator and peered inside. She pulled out a carton of milk, poured some into a pan and set it on the stove.

While she was heating the milk for hot chocolate, she found a package of crackers and a jar of peanut butter. If she were going to be wide awake, she might as well eat, she thought logically. This would be her breakfast. Lexi knew she wouldn't have much time in the morning. With her mother gone, the full responsibility of getting her handicapped brother ready for school would fall upon her shoulders.

As Lexi sat at the counter spreading peanut butter on the crackers, she thought about her grandfather. Dear, sweet Grandpa Carson was one of the best grandparents in the entire world.

He was the one who had run patiently behind her on her first bike, until she'd learned to maneuver the two-wheeler on her own. Grandpa Carson spoiled her royally, sneaking off with her after Sunday dinner to buy ice-cream cones or chocolate shakes. Grandpa Carson had taught Lexi to play chess and checkers, and to carve a whistle from a piece of wood.

When she was younger and everyone was distracted with Ben and his special care, it was Grandpa Carson who always had time for her. He was always willing to read a story, sing a song or color in the coloring books Lexi laid on his knees.

Tears streamed down Lexi's cheeks. With a snuffle, she wiped her eyes. She was suddenly very frightened and alone.

She'd meant to write to Grandpa and Grandma Carson all week long. She'd even considered calling them on the telephone. It had been a long time since she'd seen either of her grandparents.

A terrible burden of guilt settled over Lexi. She'd become so busy with school and friends since her family had moved to Cedar River that she'd hardly thought of her grandparents. Now she wished she'd taken more time for them.

Her first days at Cedar River had been so full of turmoil and trouble with Minda Hannaford and the Hi-Fives that her grandparents had hardly entered her mind. Later, when things had settled down, she'd met her friend Todd Winston. Now, with all her new friends, her job at her father's veterinary clinic, her part in the Emerald Tones choir and her position as photographer for the Cedar River High School newspaper kept her so busy she rarely thought of her grandparents.

Lexi pushed away the crackers and the cocoa. They tasted bitter and unpleasant as she considered Grandpa's sudden illness.

"I thought you were always going to be there, Grandpa," she said aloud. "I never thought about anything happening to you." Lexi lay her head on the counter feeling sad, frightened and guilty all at once.

Grandpa had *always* seemed old to her, ever since she was a little girl. He never changed. Lexi assumed that he would always be there for her. She'd taken her grandfather for granted and now. . . .

Morosely, Lexi cleared away her dishes and walked to her bedroom. She didn't want Ben to wake up and see her. Not like this. Not with tears in her eyes and a knot in her throat so large that it was choking her.

In her room, Lexi turned on all the lights, wishing the brightness would chase away the sad thoughts she was having. She crawled into bed still wearing her robe and slippers and curled into a tight little ball. Tears squeezed from beneath her eyelashes and fell silently onto her pillow. Then she remembered her fathers words: "You can pray."

Lexi reached for the Bible on her night stand. It, too, had been a gift from her grandfather and grandmother. Sometimes Lexi thought about getting a new Bible, one that wasn't so tattered and worn. This one was marked with underlined verses that meant something special to her. She loved this Bible. It had been her help through many times of trouble.

She opened the Bible to the New Testament and began to read, waiting for her "old friend" to give her words of comfort.

A coldness descended around her as she read. The words seemed jumbled and meaningless. Lexi turned to her favorite passages in Romans. Even they didn't speak to her as she had expected they would. Though she was reading, her heart did not hear.

Lexi had always believed that when she turned to the Bible for help, it would be there for her. The Lord's words had always reached out to soothe and comfort her. But tonight there was no comfort to be found, no healing. Instead, there was an icy shell around Lexi's heart which would not allow the words of comfort to penetrate.

After twenty frustrating minutes, Lexi closed the Bible and returned it to her bedside stand. She decided not to read tonight, but to do what her father had asked. To pray.

Lexi had prayed in many ways—standing up, sitting down or lounging lazily across the couch in the living room. She always spoke to God as if she were carrying on a conversation with a friend. It had never mattered how or where she prayed.

Tonight, however, was different. Lexi slid off her bed and dropped to her knees. Resting her elbows on the side of the bed, she cupped her forehead in her hands.

"I don't know what's going on here tonight, God," Lexi prayed frankly. "Grandfather's sick and I know my parents are afraid he won't live. Help him, God. Take care of my grandfather. You know what is best for him.

"Take care of my parents, too. They're driving in the middle of the night, and they're as worried as I am. I pray that you will help them get to my grandfather safely. Tomorrow help me to make Ben understand what is happening without frightening him. He's so little, Father. Because he's handicapped, it's not going to be easy for him to understand what's happening to Grandpa." Lexi paused for a long moment, thinking about what she had prayed. Then, burying her face into the mattress, she prayed for herself.

"Help me, God. Forgive me for neglecting my grandparents since we moved to Cedar River. Forgive me for thinking that they'd always be here for me, that I could always spend time with them later when I wasn't busy. I'm sure they've been lonesome, God."

Tears soaked the sheet. "Oh, God, I'm so sorry. Help my grandfather. Help our family. . . ." Lexi's voice trailed away as she lifted her head to stare out the window into the still-dark night.

Her prayers felt different tonight.

"Are you listening to me, God? Are you hearing me tonight?"

For the first time, Lexi wasn't quite sure. The cold shell of icy guilt around her heart gripped even more tightly.

"Time to get up, Ben." Lexi nudged her little brother's shoulder. "Come on, Sleepyhead. I've got breakfast all ready."

Ben opened his brown eyes and squinted sleepily at Lexi. "You cooked breakfast?" he said in groggy amazement.

"I sure did. I've got oatmeal and toast and juice. Come on, I've got your clothes all laid out."

Ben rolled to the side of the bed and dangled his feet over the edge. His pink toes wiggled several inches above the carpet. "Where's Mom?" he asked suspiciously. "How come you're waking me up today?"

"Mom had to go somewhere. I'm supposed to get you ready for school. You'll have to hurry."

Lexi prodded at her little brother, but Ben was not about to be rushed. He trudged to the bathroom.

"I don't think you have the time to take a shower this morning, Ben," Lexi said. She eyed the cowlicks that sent Ben's dark, silky hair in every direction. "Maybe we can wet your hair down to keep it from standing on end."

Ben clapped his hands over his head. "No. I don't want my head wet. Where's Mom?"

Without answering him, Lexi coaxed him into his clothes and downstairs to the breakfast table. Ben was grumpily spooning oatmeal into his mouth when Lexi sat down across from him. "Ben, I have to tell you where Mom and Dad are. They've gone to Oxford City."

Ben's almond-shaped eyes widened. "Without us?" One corner of his lip turned downward and he looked as though he were about to cry. Ben, who suffered from Down's syndrome, was a very tender little boy. The idea of being left behind upset him a great deal.

Lexi grabbed Ben's hand and squeezed it tightly. "It was an emergency, Ben. Grandpa Carson got sick last night. They had to go see him in the hospital."

"Grandpa's sick? Does he have a cold?"

"No," Lexi shook her head sadly. "It's more serious than that. Grandpa's had a stroke."

Ben stared at her blankly. "Is that bad?"

Lexi nodded. "I'm afraid it is, Ben. I thought maybe Mom or Dad would have called by now to let us know how he's doing."

Ben pushed away his bowl of oatmeal and leaned forward intently. His eyes were riveted on Lexi. "Is Grandpa going to die?"

Lexi was startled. "Why do you ask that, Ben?"

"Because my friend Robbie's puppy died. He got hit by a car."

"Well, having a stroke and getting hit by a car aren't quite the same thing, Ben, but they're both very serious."

"They buried Robbie's puppy in the ground," Ben announced.

This conversation was making Lexi uncomfortable.

"Where do people go when they die?" Ben inquired, his young voice matter-of-fact.

"Well, they go to heaven, of course."

Ben thought about that possibility for a long time. "Do they see Jesus?"

"When the time comes, I'm sure Grandpa will see Jesus."

"Oh." Ben chewed at his lower lip. "Is that where Robbie's puppy is?"

Lexi tried to distract Ben, but he would have none of it.

"Does Grandpa's tummy hurt?" he wondered.

"I don't know, Ben."

"When he got sick, did he cry?"

"I don't know that either." Lexi was afraid that if Ben didn't quit asking questions, she was going to break right down and bawl in front of him. That wouldn't do either of them any good.

Chapter Two

Lexi was thankful when the telephone rang. She hurried to pick up the receiver.

"Lexi, honey, it's Mom."

"How's Grandpa?" Lexi asked breathlessly.

Her mother was silent for a long moment. "There's been no change yet, Lexi. Grandpa's very, very ill. We've been at the hospital all night."

"Oh, I'm sorry," Lexi's voice trailed away.

"Have you got Ben ready for school?" her mother asked, trying to sound cheerful.

"He's just finishing his breakfast. He's driving me crazy asking a million questions about Grandpa."

"Let me talk to him. Maybe I can help you out."

Lexi gladly turned Ben and the telephone over to her mother. She cleared the dishes while Ben talked.

Ben hung up the phone and announced, "Mom said she'll call you after school. She said to say goodbye. She loves you."

"Thanks for the message, Ben," Lexi said with a teary smile. "Maybe you'd better run and get your jacket now. We'll have to leave early if I'm going to get you to the Academy before I go to school."

Ben nodded obediently and went to retrieve his

windbreaker. While he was in the other room, the doorbell rang. Lexi threw the door open to find her best friend Jennifer Golden and her mother standing on the steps.

"Lexi, are you all right?" Mrs. Golden asked. "I'm sorry we didn't get here earlier. I'll drive Ben to school."

At that moment, Ben came meandering into the kitchen wearing his windbreaker. His schoolbag was slung over one shoulder. "Hi, Mrs. Golden," he said with a bright smile.

"Hello, Benjamin." Mrs. Golden kneeled down to Ben's height. "Would you like to have a ride to school today? I'd be happy to take you."

Ben looked to Lexi for permission before answering, "Sure."

"Good boy." Mrs. Golden gave him a brief hug. "Come on then." She looked around the kitchen at the dirty dishes and the clutter on the counter. "Why don't we let Lexi and Jennifer stay here and do the breakfast dishes. They can walk to school. You and I will go right now."

Ben gave Lexi a smile and a wave as he followed Mrs. Golden out the door.

"You can come to our house after school, Lexi," Mrs. Golden said. "I'll pick Ben up at the Academy. Don't worry about him a bit."

"Thank you," Lexi said. "I really appreciate this."

Mrs. Golden smiled understandingly. "It's the least I can do, Lexi. We all hope and pray that your Grandfather will be all right."

After they had gone, Jennifer began clearing the dirty dishes from the table. "I hate doing dishes at home," she said bluntly. "But I guess it's all right to do them here. Just don't tell my Mom that."

Lexi opened the dishwasher and began to empty it. "Thanks. I can use all the help I can get this morning."

"Bad night?" Jennifer murmured sympathetically.

Lexi nodded. "After my parents left, it seemed like hours before I fell asleep again. It felt like I'd been sleeping ten minutes when the alarm clock rang." She ran the back of her hand over her eyes. "I don't know how I'm going to pay attention in school today."

Jennifer grinned impishly. "Who pays attention? I don't. Look how well I do."

Lexi knew better. Jennifer suffered from dyslexia. She had to pay careful attention in order to get the kind of grades she did.

———————

"It feels good to be outside," Lexi said, as they walked down the sidewalk toward Cedar River High School. She tipped her head to allow the sun's warming rays to bathe her face. "Funny how you begin to appreciate someone or something when you realize it might be taken away."

"He's that bad, then?" Jennifer asked, frowning.

Lexi nodded. "I'm afraid so. My parents haven't said it in so many words, but I can hear it in Mother's voice. I don't think that Grandpa's going to live."

Jennifer gave an empty pop can on the sidewalk a vicious kick. It went spinning and skittering down the street. "I hate it that people have to get old!"

Lexi was startled by the manner in which Jennifer spoke. "I do too. But I guess there's nothing we can do about it."

"It's not fair. I think God should have planned it some other way."

"Why do you say that?"

"I remember when my grandmother died. She was the neatest person in the entire world, Lexi. There was nobody like her. When I had trouble reading, she never lost her patience with me. She always told me, 'Someday you're going to learn how, Jennifer. It's just going to take you a little more time.' She spoiled me every way she could. She baked cookies for me and knitted sweaters, and," Jennifer's voice wavered, "I still miss her."

Lexi stubbed the toes of her tennis shoes on the sidewalk as she walked. "I never really thought about it much before," she admitted. "Teenagers don't usually think about getting old or dying. It's like death happens to somebody else in some other world."

"Well, teenagers die too sometimes," Jennifer pointed out. "Like in car accidents or suicides, or. . . ."

"True, but it's usually an accident. It's different when people get *old*." Lexi had begun to hate the word.

"I wish my Mom and Dad were young like yours," Jennifer said suddenly.

"What do you mean by that?" Lexi asked. "Your Mom and Dad *are* young."

"They're not as young as your parents. My mother was close to forty when I was born. That means they'll be old a whole lot sooner than your parents will." Jennifer stared straight ahead, her expression tense. "I worry about it sometimes. What if the same thing that happened to my grandmother happens to them?"

"Not for a long, long time," Lexi assured her. "Your mom looks great to me. I didn't realize she was older than my mom."

"You didn't?" Jennifer brightened. "That's good." She smiled and some of the old Jennifer returned. "I'm being silly worrying about things I can't do anything about anyway."

"I hadn't thought much about any of this until last night." Lexi gave a shudder. "You know what really scared me, Jen? It was thinking about my grandfather dying and realizing that I haven't seen him for a long time. I haven't told him that I love him." Her voice trailed away. "I hate this."

Jennifer nodded in understanding. "After my grandma died, I didn't want to be around old people anymore."

"Why?"

"They scare me, that's all." She looked embarrassed. "I know, it sounds dumb, but it's the truth. It scares me to be around old people."

They walked together for a few moments in silence before Jennifer continued. "Have you ever noticed old people's hands?" She held out her own smooth, pink hands for Lexi's examination. "They always have those puffy blue lines in them that stand up on the skin." She shuddered. "Or they're covered with those icky brown spots. My mother says they're called 'liver spots.' Can you imagine? How gross!"

"They can't help that anymore than Ben can help having Down's syndrome."

"No, I suppose not," Jennifer said. "But it bothers me anyway. And sometimes old people don't have any teeth."

Lexi gave a half smile. "My grandfather doesn't. He keeps his false ones in a glass while he sleeps at night."

"Oh, gross!" Jennifer said with another shudder. "I don't even want to think about it."

"Well, you better brush and floss," Lexi muttered bluntly.

"It's not funny," Jennifer blurted. "When I was little, we had a neighbor who was old. Really old. She went to the beauty salon and had her hair dyed blue."

"Blue hair?"

"Sometimes it came out purple." Jennifer made a face. "And she always smelled like stale perfume. Her eyesight wasn't very good. When you went into her house you could see the dust and cobwebs hanging from the ceiling. She couldn't see it though, so she never dusted or cleaned."

"Maybe she needed better glasses," Lexi said. "Even young people can have poor eyesight."

"And she had cats," Jennifer continued. "About six of them."

"So? Lots of people have cats."

"Not like these. They crawled all over everything. On her counters, in her oven, in her sink. They were everywhere. She never scolded them. She called them her 'pretties.'"

"Just because you knew one person like that

doesn't mean that all older people are that way," Lexi pointed out.

"Maybe," Jennifer said, "but I still think getting old is gross."

———

Gross. Is that what aging is? Lexi wondered, as she changed her books in her locker between classes. *It must be awful to be old and to have kids laugh at you and think you're strange, to not be able to use your own teeth or see without glasses.*

Lexi's conversation with Jennifer had upset her. Every time she thought about her grandfather, she felt like crying. She didn't care how old or gross her grandfather was, just as long as he was alive. Fortunately, because of her classes she didn't have much time to think about it.

———

Lexi was still feeling sad at noon when she walked through the cafeteria line and into the lunchroom. Todd Winston, Egg and Binky McNaughton, Harry Cramer and Jennifer were all waiting for her at their special table. Five pair of sympathetic eyes followed her as she walked across the room.

"Hi, how're you doing?" Egg asked.

"Sorry to hear about your grandfather," Harry said. "That's really tough."

Todd simply reached across the table and grabbed Lexi's hand, giving it a gentle squeeze.

"What do the doctors say?" Egg asked.

"I don't know. There will probably be news tonight when I get home. He's not very well." Lexi answered.

Binky, who was tenderhearted and emotional, looked at Lexi with tear-filled eyes. "I feel so sorry for you," she whimpered.

"Thanks guys. Just knowing you care makes me feel a whole lot better." Lexi took the sloppy joe sandwich and potato chips from her tray. "Let's not talk about it anymore for a while. Okay?" Tears sprang to her eyes. "I don't think I can take much more of it."

Quickly the conversation turned to topics that might cheer Lexi, including the new music the Emerald Tones were rehearsing for concert and Minda Hannaford's very latest fashion recommendation— neon—for her column in the *River Review*. No matter how cheerfully they talked, however, Lexi's problem was still foremost in their minds.

In a quiet moment, Harry murmured, "You know, Lexi, I could drive Ben to the Academy in the morning if Mrs. Golden doesn't have time."

"That's awful nice of you, Harry," Lexi said.

Harry Cramer really was a great guy. He and Binky McNaughton had become an "item" lately. Lexi was delighted for her friend. She was glad that Binky had someone special in her life. After all, Lexi had Todd. Just then, he slipped his arm around Lexi's shoulders and gave her a compassionate squeeze.

There was a lull in the conversation. Binky, who always spoke whatever was on her mind commented, "I wonder why it happens."

"Why what happens?" someone asked.

"Why people get sick. Why people get old."

"Good question," Harry muttered. "Seems like it'd be easier if everyone stayed young."

"Yeah," Binky said indignantly. "Old age is a mean trick God plays on people's lives." Her face got pink. "If God created us, why does He let us get old and get sick?"

Todd, who'd been quiet through much of the conversation, finally spoke up, "Well, it's not really God's trick, Binky. It's our own trick. Man's trick. We did it to ourselves. There's a verse in the Bible that says something like this, "Therefore as sin entered the world through one man and death through sin, and so death spread to all men because all men sinned. . . .""

"You mean God didn't plan it for us?"

Todd shook his head. "We brought it upon ourselves. God didn't give us sin. Man went out and found it for himself. That's the story of Adam and Eve."

Binky scratched her head. "It's all too deep for me. I'm not smart like you are, Todd."

Todd chuckled. "You don't have to be smart to have faith, Binky. Anyone can have faith."

Lexi listened to the conversation, but did not speak. She felt strange, as if a glass wall were dividing her from Todd and the rest of her friends. She knew that what Todd was saying was true. She'd heard it all of her life. But, today, for the first time, it was difficult to accept.

It wasn't right that the people she loved got sick! Having a retarded brother was bad enough. Now Grandpa, whom she loved so much, was ill. Lexi couldn't understand it.

She shivered. There was a cold, scary feeling growing inside her. It was though the news about Grandpa had done something to her heart, hardening it a little.

After lunch, Todd and Lexi walked together down the hall. Todd put his arm around her. "Let me know if there's any change in your grandfather's condition." He gave her a hug. "I'll be praying for you, Lex."

She stared after him as he sauntered to his next class. Todd was going to pray for her. She should be appreciative, Lexi knew, but she didn't feel that way at all. Instead, she felt angry. Angry that her grandfather was sick. Angry that God wasn't helping her to understand all that was going on.

Lexi went to her locker. With a rough jerk, she pulled out the books she needed for her next class. The entire contents of her locker spilled onto the floor and scattered in ten directions. "Oh, no," she cried aloud. "I'll be late for class."

Two students passing by bent to help her retrieve her belongings. With a quick "thank you" she stuffed them back into her locker and ran down the hall.

I'll pray for you. Todd had said. *Well, he'd better get started*, Lexi thought as she flung herself into her desk. Todd had better pray fast and hard. Something was happening to her. Lexi was feeling something that she'd never felt before. She felt angry—with God.

Chapter Three

"Are you going to the Hamburger Shack?" Binky asked after the last class of the day. "Harry and I thought we'd have a malt."

"I don't think so," Lexi said, shaking her head. "I feel kind of funny today. I think I'd feel better if I could talk to my parents. I'll go home and wait for them to call."

"I don't blame you," Binky said. "There's always another day for the Hamburger Shack."

Lexi and Jennifer walked together in silence toward Jennifer's home. Though it was a beautiful afternoon and the sun was shining, Lexi felt dark and gloomy.

"Looks like my Mom's home," Jennifer said, seeing a car in the driveway. "I thought she'd be picking up Ben about now."

Lexi looked at her watch. "Today's the day that Ben stays after school. He's on a team that practices until five. They're already in training for the Special Olympics."

The two girls walked to the back of the house and entered by the garage door. As Lexi stepped into the kitchen, she felt a strange sensation along the back of her neck, as if the fine hairs were standing on end. "Something's wrong," she whispered to Jennifer.

Jennifer looked around, her expression blank. "No, I don't think so. Why do you say that?"

"It's so quiet."

Jennifer tipped her head. "I can hear music playing in the other room. It's just your overactive imagination, Lexi, that's all."

When Mrs. Golden came to the kitchen door, Lexi's stomach tied in a huge, nervous knot. Something *was* wrong. She could tell by the look on Jennifer's mother's face.

"Lexi, would you come into the living room for a minute?" Mrs. Golden said softly.

Lexi nodded and followed her.

"Sit down, dear," Mrs. Golden said gently.

Lexi dropped onto the couch and stared at her friend's mother. *What is going on?*

"Lexi, I'm terribly sorry to be the one to tell you this, but, your parents called about an hour ago. Your grandfather has passed away."

Lexi stared at Mrs. Golden, her lips pressed together in a tight line. "What?"

"Your grandfather has died, Lexi. I'm so sorry."

"But—but—" Lexi stammered, at a loss for words.

"He died in his sleep. Your mother said it was a real blessing that he didn't suffer anymore."

Lexi stared at Mrs. Golden. "A blessing that he's dead?" Adults had the strangest way of thinking about things! Her grandfather was dead and people thought it was a blessing? Anger, grief and a frightening sort of sadness welled up in Lexi.

"No!" She stood up, her fists clenched tightly together at her waist. "No! He's not dead."

"I'm sorry, Lexi, but your mother. . . ."

"I haven't said goodbye to Grandpa yet. He *can't* be dead. I don't believe you."

Suddenly, the telephone rang. Jennifer raced to pick it up. "Hello. Goldens'," she said with a sort of quiet panic in her voice. She held the phone out to Lexi. "It's for you. It's your mom."

Woodenly, Lexi crossed the room to where Jennifer stood. "Hello? Mom?"

"Lexi, did Mrs. Golden tell you?"

"She did, Mom, but I don't believe her. Grandpa can't be dead."

"I'm sorry, honey. He died very quietly. He was in no pain. It was really quite wonderful. He's with the Lord now."

"He can't be dead."

"I know it's hard for you to accept, Lexi. And I'm sure it's more difficult because you weren't here with us. I'm sorry I'm not there to talk to you and hold you for a little while, but we're coming home soon. We'll return to Cedar River tonight, and then bring you and Ben back for the funeral."

The funeral. It sounded so final. But hearing her mother's voice calmed Lexi. "Mom, how's Grandma?" Lexi wondered. She'd hardly thought about her grandmother in the past hours because she'd been so concerned about her grandfather. *Poor Grandmother. She and Grandpa were very close. What must it be like for her?*

"Grandma is. . . ." Mrs. Leighton was quiet for a long time on the other end of the line.

"Mom? Are you there?"

"Yes, Lexi. Grandma isn't feeling very well right now."

"You mean she's sick like Grandpa?" A note of panic crept into Lexi's voice.

"Oh, no, nothing like that. Grandma's just confused."

Confused? That didn't make any sense at all. Grandma Carson was the sharpest, most "with it" grandma Lexi had ever met. When hem lines changed, Grandma Carson's changed too. When Lexi came to visit, Grandma would have a tape of recent popular music playing on her tape player. She always kept up on the latest news and wanted to discuss current events with Lexi. There was not a confused bone in Grandma Carson's body!

"How can that be, Mom?" Lexi stammered. "You know Grandma."

"Yes, honey, I know. We're hoping that once the funeral is over and she can get back to her normal activity things will be better for her. This has been very hard on her. I'm praying that everything will return to normal."

Lexi was alarmed by the tone of her mother's voice. She sounded frightened. Parents weren't supposed to be frightened! They were supposed to be strong for their children, no matter what happened.

"Should I tell Ben about Grandpa?" Lexi ventured, hoping that her mother would say no.

"That may be too hard for you, Lexi. It will be tough to explain to him that his grandpa's gone. Your dad and I will handle it when we get home."

"Mom, I. . . ." Lexi wanted to express some of the

things she was feeling in her head and in her heart, but she couldn't find the words.

"Yes, Lexi," her mother tried to encourage her. "What is it, dear?"

"Tell Grandmother I love her."

"All right, honey, I will. We'll be home soon. Don't worry now."

"Good-bye, Mom."

"Good-bye, Lexi."

Slowly Lexi replaced the receiver. "It's true. Grandpa's dead," Lexi said softly to Jennifer. It didn't make sense to her. The last time she'd seen Grandpa, he'd been playing kickball with Ben on the front lawn. That image simply did not match the one her mother had given her of Grandpa in a hospital, dying.

Mrs. Golden stood up. "Are you girls going to be all right if I leave to pick up Ben at the Academy?"

Lexi nodded, fresh tears coming to her eyes. "I'll be all right. Jennifer's here with me. If you don't mind, I'll just stay upstairs in Jennifer's room when Ben gets here. If he sees me, he's going to know that something is wrong."

"Of course, dear. I can keep Ben busy in the kitchen. Perhaps we can make some cookies."

Lexi moved toward the staircase leading to Jennifer's room. Jennifer, at a loss for words, followed quietly.

In the bedroom, Lexi flung herself against the headboard with such force that it trembled.

"I can't believe it. I just can't believe it," she said angrily. "Grandpa—gone!"

"I know it's hard, but. . . ."

"You know?" Lexi said sarcastically. "How can you know how I feel, Jennifer?"

"I can just imagine, Lexi. . . ."

"Imagining doesn't make it real," Lexi said angrily. She punched her fists into the fluffy pillow. Tears streamed down her face. "I never knew it'd be like this."

"Oh, Lexi. . . ." Jennifer stood in the doorway helplessly, her hands drooped to her sides, her eyes betraying her anguish.

"I'm sorry, Jennifer," Lexi said contritely, "I shouldn't have yelled at you. You were just trying to help. It's just that I feel so angry inside and so mad I can't explain it. I'm furious! He shouldn't have died, Jennifer. Not without my getting to say goodbye."

"Try not to think about the fact that you didn't say goodbye, Lexi. Remember the good times that you spent with your grandfather. You loved him a lot. And he loved you."

Lexi paced the room like a tiger in a small cage. "I can't, Jennifer. All I remember are the things that I did wrong."

"Wrong? You?" Jennifer looked confused. "I didn't think you ever did anything wrong."

Lexi gave her a cross look. "This is no time to joke, Jennifer. The last time we went to visit Grandma and Grandpa, he wanted to give me a box of chocolates that he'd bought for me at the store. Do you know what I did? I said 'no,' because they'd make me fat."

"So?" Jennifer looked at her friend blankly. "What does that have to do with anything?"

"I said 'no' to him, Jennifer. He'd been so kind

and so good. He went to the store to buy me something and I refused to take it. What kind of a person would do that?"

"A person who is watching her weight. A person who didn't like chocolates. It doesn't mean you didn't love your grandfather," Jennifer said matter-of-factly.

"And he called two or three weeks ago and asked me when I was coming to see him. I just laughed and said, 'Oh, I don't know, Grandpa, I'm really busy.' I told him about the Emerald Tones and the photography I was doing for the *River Review* and I never did tell him when I'd come to see him." Lexi's voice rose to a panicked pitch. "Maybe there was something I could have said or done that might have helped him."

"You mean you think that something you could have said or done would have kept him from dying?" Jennifer asked bluntly. "Don't kid yourself, Lexi. That's not possible. Your grandfather was old and sick."

"He was old and lonely. It's my fault that he was lonely."

"He had your grandmother," Jennifer pointed out.

Lexi sank onto the bed and cradled her head in her hands. She was stunned by all the hurt and the anger churning inside her. "Oh, Jennifer. You're right. Your words *sound* right, but it's just not what I feel. I feel so sad and so guilty. There must have been *something* I could have done."

"You were a terrific grandchild, Lexi. You loved your grandparents. What more could you do?"

Lexi's tears still splashed onto the bedspread. "I don't know. Something. Anything."

"Something happened inside your grandfather's body. You could have gone to see him every day. You could have eaten all the chocolates in the world. It still wouldn't have stopped this."

"I suppose you're right, Jennifer." Lexi drew a ragged breath. "I'm sorry I yelled at you."

"Hey, I can take a lot of grief. I've given plenty." Jennifer sat down on the bed and gave Lexi a huge squeeze.

Lexi felt herself trembling in her friend's arms. She snuffled and gave Jennifer a weak grin. "You've got a great shoulder to cry on, Jen."

Jennifer mopped at her shoulder. "Yeah, and now it's a soggy one, too. Lexi, maybe you'd feel better if you talked to Todd."

Todd! Lexi had forgotten all about telling Todd. She knew he'd want to know what had happened. "I'll do that."

"Why don't I go downstairs and wait for Mom to bring Ben home. Maybe I can distract him for a little while."

"Thanks, Jen. You're a real friend."

Jennifer shrugged her shoulders and didn't say anything more. Her eyes were wide and looked worried as she closed the door, leaving Lexi alone in the bedroom.

Chapter Four

Lexi dialed Todd's telephone number. It rang three times before his rich, cheerful voice came on the line. "Hello, Winston residence, Todd speaking."

"Todd?"

"Lexi? Is that you? You sound funny. Are you all right?"

"He died, Todd. He died in his sleep."

There was a long silence on the other end of the line. When Todd spoke, his voice was rough with sadness. "I'm sorry, I really am."

"Mom and Dad are coming home tonight to tell Ben and to take us back to Oxford City for the funeral."

"Is there anything I can do?" Todd wondered.

"Just talk to me, Todd." Lexi clung to the phone as though it were a lifeline. "Just talk to me."

"Why don't *you* talk to me?" Todd said wisely. "Tell me how you feel, Lexi."

"How I'm feeling? Pretty awful."

"That's normal," Todd said softly.

"I feel sad and mad and guilty, like I should have done or said something to stop this. I should have visited Grandpa more often. And I'm angry. I'm really angry, Todd," Lexi blurted, surprising even herself. "How could Grandpa do this? How could he leave us? When I was little, I thought Grandpa was going to be here forever. Now he's gone. Just gone. There's no more of him."

"He couldn't help it, Lexi. He wouldn't choose to leave you."

"Then what's wrong with God? Why did He do this to me? Why did He do this to our family? He knows how much we love our grandfather!"

"Lexi, this doesn't sound like you," Todd said anxiously.

"I just don't understand it Todd. If it's not Grandpa's fault and it's not my fault, whose fault is it? It has to be God's."

"God doesn't wish sad or evil things on us, Lexi. You know that as well as I do. Man has brought death upon himself. Besides, your grandfather is with God. He's all right. It's everybody who is left behind who's feeling miserable."

Lexi knew that what Todd said was true. It was what she had believed all her life. But now, in the face of Grandpa's death, it didn't seem to make much sense. Nothing made sense anymore.

"I'm sorry I'm so angry, Todd. I don't know what's gotten into me," Lexi apologized. "I shouldn't have yelled at you."

"Hey, I'm here for you, Lexi. Anytime you need me. You know that."

Tears threatened to overwhelm her again. "I'd better go, Todd. My parents will be here soon."

"Call me when you get back from the funeral. Will you do that? Promise?"

As she hung up the phone, Lexi felt a strange coldness rolling over her. It was as though something had snapped inside her. Something very precious had broken and she didn't know if it could be repaired. Silently she moved to Jennifer's bed, laid on the edge and curled up into a tight ball. "Grandpa, oh, Grandpa," she moaned. The tears finally came full force. Lexi cried until she fell asleep.

She awoke suddenly to the sound of slamming doors and voices downstairs. Lexi glanced in the mirror at her reddened eyes and puffy cheeks before descending the staircase to greet her parents.

Lexi's mother was standing in the hallway. Her eyes were red too, and Lexi knew she had been crying. Without a word, Mrs. Leighton gathered Lexi into her arms.

"Have you told Ben yet?" Lexi asked.

"Your father's talking to him right now," Mrs. Leighton said. "Poor little guy. He'll take this hard."

Mr. Leighton and Ben came walking into the foyer from the kitchen. Mr. Leighton looked tired and sad. Ben looked curious.

"Ben, come here, honey," Mrs. Leighton said. She gathered her little son into her arms. "Are you okay?"

"I'm fine," Ben said cheerfully. "Are we going to go see Grandpa now?" he wondered.

Mrs. Leighton looked from Lexi to her husband. "You might say that, Ben. We're going to his funeral."

"Grandpa's going to be there?"

"The funeral is for him, Ben. Grandpa died."

"He'll come back, won't he? He'll come back for

the—" Ben stammered, "fu-ner-al."

"No, honey. Grandpa isn't coming back. Didn't Daddy tell you?"

Ben shook his head stubbornly. "Grandpa will be back. He always comes back."

Mrs. Golden laid her hand on Mrs. Leighton's arm. "Maybe Ben is hoping that if he pretends this hasn't happened it won't be real. It will take time to sink in."

Lexi looked at her little brother sadly. Poor Ben. He didn't understand why this happened anymore than she did. He had faith that Grandpa would be coming back. Lexi knew otherwise. A twinge of guilt assailed her.

Where was her faith now that she talked about so much? Faith that assured her that her Grandpa would be back someday, that he would rise from the dead when Christ returned. Lexi clutched her fingers into tight fists. Right now she didn't care about the resurrection day. She wanted Grandpa here. Now. With her and Ben.

———

Would the drive to Oxford City ever end? Lexi wondered as she stared morosely out the car window at the passing scenery. Would her little brother ever quit asking questions? One moment Ben would assure his entire family that Grandpa would be back in time for the funeral and the next moment he would torment Lexi with questions about death, about the deep and painful things that he couldn't understand.

Lexi knew it was difficult for Ben to understand

that Grandfather had died. She felt the same way. Still, the questions he kept asking just about drove her wild. She rode numbly, listening with one ear to the conversation, her mind whirling with confused thoughts.

"Why did Grandpa go to see Jesus?" Ben asked curiously. "Why didn't he want to stay here with Grandma?"

"We don't know why this was Grandpa's time to go, Ben," his mother said, "but we know that Jesus will take good care of him. Grandpa wasn't feeling very well. Now, in heaven, he's going to feel just fine. People who are living with Jesus don't have any pain and they're very, very happy. Would you like to know more about Jesus, Ben? Would you like to talk to Him?"

Lexi felt like covering her ears and screaming. In her head she knew that Grandpa was better off in God's presence than here on earth. Still, she wanted to be able to talk to him, to hold him, to laugh with him. Her head told her one thing and her heart told her quite another.

"Here we are," Mr. Leighton announced, as they pulled into the grandparents' driveway. "The old house looks just the same, doesn't it?"

Lexi stared at the big, white three-story house with the gabled roof. It did look the same. It wasn't the same, however, not inside. Grandpa wasn't there anymore.

While her parents unpacked the car, Lexi stared at the house, thinking of the happy days of her childhood and the many wonderful hours she'd spent under that roof.

There was the big old tree from which she and Grandfather used to hang birdhouses. They built them in his basement out of rough scraps of lumber. Sometimes Grandpa would allow Lexi to design what she called "bird condominiums." They were clumsy, awkwardly made things, but the birds seemed to love them.

By the kitchen window hung one of Grandpa's many hummingbird feeders. He loved the tiny, darting birds that came to sip sugar water from the brightly colored feeders. Their tiny wings beat so rapidly that they were only a blur. Grandpa had had a way with hummingbirds.

She thought of the afternoons she and Grandpa had shared in the kitchen eating Grandpa's raw potato sandwiches and drinking lemonade. The only time she ever ate a raw potato sandwich was at Grandpa's house. He knew how to slice the potatoes thinly and spread lots of butter over the bread and add salt and pepper. She could almost taste one of his sandwiches now, crisp and sweet and unlike anything else in the whole world.

"Lexi, do you want to carry this bag inside?" Her father thrust a suitcase into her hands.

As Lexi mounted the front steps, her heart gave a lurch. As clearly as if it were yesterday, Lexi could see herself with braids and skinned knees, sitting on the front steps of the house, playing stone school with Grandpa.

He would gather together all the children in the neighborhood and settle them on the bottom step. Then Grandpa would find a small stone or pebble and secure it in a hand behind his back, moving the stone from one hand to the other until no one knew which hand held the stone. Then he would hold his tightly closed hands out in front of him.

Each of the children would guess which hand held the stone. If they guessed correctly, they were allowed to move upward one step. The first one to reach the top step graduated from stone school. That child became the teacher for the next game. Grandpa would cheerfully find his way to the bottom step to become a pupil at the school.

Lexi settled her suitcase on the steps for a minute and held her hands tightly over her chest. It was as though she could feel her heart breaking, shattering into a million little pieces.

"Come on, Lexi," Ben said, interrupting her thoughts. "Grandma's inside."

Lexi pulled herself together. Ben was right, absolutely right. Grandmother was inside. Lexi was eager to see her.

At least she still had Grandmother to rely on.

Chapter Five

Ben stood inside the enclosed front porch of his grandparents' home asking questions.

"If Grandpa's dead, is Grandma going to die, too?" Ben asked innocently.

His eyes were large and fearful. "And if Grandma dies, are you and Daddy going to die, too?" He looked at his mother with concern.

Mrs. Leighton kneeled down and gave Ben a hug. "It's scary, isn't it, Ben? You start to wonder who'll be left to take care of you."

Ben nodded somberly.

"Don't worry. Just because Grandpa died doesn't mean that anyone else will. We're going to be with you every day. If, when you go back to school, you start to worry about us, you can call home and talk to me. Just to make yourself feel a little better."

"I can?" Ben's eyes grew wide. "I can use the telephone at school?"

"Whenever you need to, Ben. But I don't think you're going to need to very often."

Ben thought about what his mother said for a long moment before announcing, "I'm never going to die."

45

Mrs. Leighton's eyebrow arched and she said, "Oh?"

"Yeah," Ben assured her. "You have to be sick before you die, so I'm never going to be sick. Then I won't die."

"Just because you get sick doesn't mean you're going to die, Ben. People get sick all the time and then they become well again."

"I won't be sick," Ben assured his mother. "Never, ever again." With that, he walked boldly into the house.

Mr. Leighton followed him, leaving Lexi alone with her mother on the porch.

"He'll learn to deal with this in time," Mrs. Leighton assured Lexi. "Ben doesn't understand what's happened right now, but his emotions are strong. I know his questions are upsetting you, but he has to attempt to grasp what's happened. You'll have to be patient with him."

"I just wish he'd quit talking about death so much!" Lexi burst out.

Mrs. Leighton put her arm around her daughter. "Small children are bound to be curious about death. They haven't learned yet that sometimes adults don't like to talk about certain subjects. I don't want to teach Ben that there are some things he can't talk to us about. So we have to answer his questions as best we can."

Lexi nodded mutely. She knew her mother was right. It was just that it hurt so much.

Together, they stepped inside. The house was perfectly unchanged from the last time Lexi had been there. The hardwood floors gleamed with a soft light.

Grandma's two parakeets chirped and fluttered contentedly in their brass cage by the front window. Lexi could smell the scents of cinnamon and lilac. There were shelves and shelves of dusty books—books that Grandpa had loved and Grandmother hated to dust. In the corner of the living room stood Grandpa's big corduroy chair. It seemed to be waiting for his return.

Lexi felt as though she'd been kicked in the stomach. Everything was so normal here. How could he be gone? Nothing else had changed. Suddenly, the sound of shattering glass jolted her back to reality.

"Oh, dear," someone cried from the kitchen.

"That's Grandma," Mrs. Leighton said with concern. "Let's find out what's happened."

Lexi followed her mother into the kitchen. Mr. Leighton and Ben were already there. Grandma stood in the middle of the room wringing her hands and staring sadly at the shattered cookie jar on the floor.

"It just slipped out of my hands," she said, putting her hands to her face. "I thought I had a better grip on it than that."

"It's all right, Mother Carson," Mr. Leighton assured her. "It's no problem. I'll grab a broom and sweep it up."

"I was *sure* I was holding it tightly. I've never done such a thing before," Grandma fussed, as if she hadn't even heard Mr. Leighton speak at all.

"Where do you keep your dustpan?" Mr. Leighton asked, but Grandma was too worried about the mess on the floor to answer him.

"The only good thing is that it wasn't full of cookies. Just a few crumbs. I wonder who ate all the cookies? It couldn't have been Fred. Fred hasn't been hungry lately."

Lexi felt a twist of pain. Fred was her grandfather. Fred and Grace Carson. Two of the dearest people on the face of the earth.

Grandma made a clucking sound under her breath and moved around the broken pieces of glass on the floor.

"Tsk, tsk, tsk," she said, clicking her tongue. "My, my, my. What a mess."

Mr. Leighton got on his knees and swept the glass into the dustpan, which he'd found on his own. When he stood up, he looked at Grandma and asked, "Where do you want me to put this Mother Carson? Do you have a garbage can somewhere?"

Grandma, who until that moment had been totally absorbed with the broken jar on the floor, looked at her son-in-law with a strangely blank stare. "Well, young man, if you didn't know where the garbage can was, why did you sweep up?"

Lexi frowned. She'd never heard Grandma Carson call her father a 'young man' before. She'd always called him Jim. In fact, for a moment it seemed to Lexi that her grandmother was looking at her dad as if she'd never seen him before in her life. Lexi's notion was confirmed when Grandma peered into his face.

"Who are you, young man? Why did you sweep up this mess? I could have done it myself."

"Mother Carson, it's me," Mr. Leighton said softly. "Jim. Marilyn's husband."

With a blink, Grandmother's head seemed to clear. "Oh my, Jim, of course. I'm sorry. How silly of me!" She wiped a hand across her eyes as if to clear cobwebs from her mind. She stared at the shards of broken glass and the dustpan. The blue eyes, which only a moment ago had seemed so blank and strange, flooded with tears. "Poor Fred," she said. "That was his favorite cookie jar." Her voice cracked with pain.

Here was someone with an ache even deeper than her own, Lexi thought. She put the suitcase she still held on the floor, and threw her arms about the old woman's thin shoulders. Grandmother, as always, smelled sweetly of cinnamon and lilacs.

As she hugged her, Lexi could feel sharp bony shoulders. It was as though she'd shrunk since the last time they'd been together.

"Oh, Grandma," she said as tears came to her eyes. "I'm so sorry about Grandpa. I'm so sorry for you."

"Grandpa?" she murmured, "You're sorry for Grandpa?" She looked at Lexi intently. "My, aren't you a big girl."

Lexi stared at her grandmother in confusion. Grandma didn't seem to remember what had happened. In fact, Grandma hardly seemed to remember her at all.

"Are you all right?" Lexi asked, fear jabbing at her heart.

"Me? Oh my, yes. I'm just fine. Clumsy, though. I never should have broken Fred's favorite cookie jar."

Before Lexi could say any more, her mother stood beside them. "Lexi, I think your grandmother is very tired. I'm sure you are too. Perhaps we should all go to bed. Your dad can finish cleaning up while I take Grandmother and Ben upstairs."

"But I want to. . . ."

"Not now, Lexi," Mrs. Leighton said firmly. "My mother is very tired. You'll have a much better conversation with her in the morning."

Grandma seemed to be in a world of her own, babbling about the broken cookie jar and the kind of cookies she'd have to bake to fill it.

Grandma *did* look tired, frail and small. It was as if in losing Grandpa she'd also lost a part of herself.

"You can sleep in my old room," Mrs. Leighton said to Lexi. "Dad and I will sleep in the guest room. Ben can sleep in his sleeping bag on the floor with us."

Lexi nodded numbly, picked up her suitcase and started for the stairs. If she weren't so exhausted, she might have resented the way her mother rushed her off to bed as though she were a little child.

Lexi heard her mother talking softly to Grandma as she helped her get ready for bed. She dropped her own clothes on the floor near the foot of the bed and slid a nightshirt over her head. Quickly she crawled into the big brass bed that had once been her mother's. She lay on her back, her hands tucked under her head and stared at the sloping ceiling.

She'd slept in this bed dozens of times. Each time she'd stayed with her grandparents had been a time filled with happy memories. Lexi studied the tiny flower print on the walls—pink and lavender sprigs with tiny green buds and leaves.

When she was much younger, she had lain in bed and attempted to count the flowers on the walls. Never once had she been able to finish counting before her eyes drooped shut and she'd fallen asleep.

If only things could be as they had been! Then everything would be perfect. After several minutes of tossing and turning, Lexi decided to resort to her childhood practice. Beginning in one corner, she focused on the flowers and counted to herself, "One, two, three, four. . . ."

By the time Lexi reached one hundred, her eyelids were feeling very heavy and her body had finally relaxed. "One hundred ninety-eight, one hundred ninety-nine, two hundred, two hundred one. . . ."

It was the first time in many years that Lexi had intentionally gone to sleep without saying her evening prayers.

———

Lexi's eyes opened slowly and she drew a deep breath. Was that bacon she smelled? The sun was shining brightly through her window and the clock on the bedside stand read eight-fifteen.

Lexi sat up and stretched like a tabby cat who'd been lying in the sun. She wiggled her toes and slid them into her slippers by the side of the bed. Suddenly she was very, very hungry.

Lexi had always loved her grandmother's cooking—especially her breakfasts, which usually consisted of bacon and eggs, fresh hot biscuits and homemade jam.

Lexi felt much better this morning. She was sure her grandmother would too. It was amazing what a night's rest could do. Surely Grandmother would not be so odd and unreachable as she had been last night.

Lexi clattered down the stairs and burst into the

kitchen. "Good morning, Grandma. The bacon smells wonderful. What else are you hav—?" Lexi skidded to a stop. Her mother stood at the stove in a white ruffled apron frying bacon and stirring hot cereal.

Grandma Carson was sitting at the kitchen table, her head bowed, plucking mindlessly at the hem of a placemat. Her hair hung loosely around her face. Her shoulders drooped. She looked unusually pale and thin in her pink cotton housecoat.

Lexi noticed the blue veins standing out on her grandmother's hands as she fingered the placemat.

"Good morning, Lexi," Mrs. Leighton said with forced cheerfulness. "How are you this morning?"

"Fine, I. . . ." Lexi's gaze darted from her mother to her grandmother and back again.

Mrs. Leighton nodded her head briefly, encouraging Lexi to speak to her grandmother.

Lexi moved closer to the table. "Good morning, Grandma. How are you today? Don't you look pretty!"

Grandma Carson didn't seem to hear. She kept picking at the ruffle on the placemat.

"I'd like to talk to you Lexi," Mr. Leighton said in a very firm voice that allowed no argument. "Come with me into the living room."

"But Grandma. . . ." Lexi stammered.

Her dad shook his head. "Into the living room, Lexi. Now."

As they left the room, he pulled his daughter close and gave her a squeeze. "I need to talk to you, honey. I think it's best if we're alone."

"What's wrong with her?" Lexi felt the panic swell and threaten to choke her.

"I know it's a shock to see Grandma this way," Mr. Leighton began. "It was very difficult for your mother too. We knew that your grandmother had been mixed-up lately. Grandpa had told us. He'd tell little jokes about her forgetting the teapot on the stove or starting the dishwasher without dishes in it. He always made a joke of it and so we didn't worry. It seems Grandpa's death has increased her confusion. We're going to have to give her a little time, Lexi. She's going to need our help to get through this."

"Time?" Lexi asked anxiously. "How much time is it going to take before she's like she used to be?"

Mr. Leighton shook his head. "I don't know, Lexi. We're very worried about her. All we can do is love and support her and get her through the next few days. After that, we'll make a decision about what to do next."

"Dad, I can't stand to see her this way! She just sits there, staring down at the floor, pulling at that placemat. That's not like Grandma."

"She's had a severe shock, Lexi," Mr. Leighton said calmly. "She needs lots of love, attention, patience and care. You'll have to help us give this to her, Lexi. This isn't the kind of thing we can just fix. It will take Grandma some time to work through her grief."

He put his hand on her shoulders and looked into her eyes. "I understand that this is difficult, Lexi, but your mother and I are counting on you. You're a very mature, sensible young woman. If you see Grandmother behave in ways you're not used to, just try to understand."

Lexi nodded numbly. *How could this have happened? How could Grandfather have died and left Grandma so alone and confused? Surely someone somewhere could have done something!*

When Lexi returned to the kitchen, her mother was serving up the bacon and eggs. Grandmother sat at the table with her eyes closed, humming a lullaby that Lexi recalled from her childhood. Whenever Lexi was tired or afraid, Grandma had held her and sung that lullaby.

It occurred to Lexi that Grandmother was holding her hands in a very odd position as she sat rocking and humming. Lexi stared at her for a long time before she realized what her grandmother was doing. She was rocking an imaginary baby in her arms.

A cold chill went through Lexi and she began to shiver. What was happening to Grandmother? What was going on?

Chapter Six

The next couple of days passed in a haze for Lexi. The door bell rang constantly as friends and neighbors came to express their sympathy to Grace Carson and her family.

Lexi stared at the kitchen countertops covered with cakes and pies, cookies and casseroles. "I've never seen so much food in my entire life."

Marilyn Leighton smiled wearily. "When someone dies, people want to help. They bring food to make sure we don't have to bother cooking meals."

"But who's hungry?" Lexi protested.

"No one, right now. We'll put most of this in Grandma's freezer. What we don't use while we're here, she can use when we go home."

"Are we going to be able to leave her?" Lexi wondered.

"She seems much better now," Mrs. Leighton said with relief in her voice. The doorbell interrupted their conversation. "Will you answer it, Lexi?"

A tall, kind-looking bald man stood on the step. He wore a dark suit and carried a Bible.

"You must be Lexi," he said without hesitation.

Lexi was surprised that he knew her name. "Yes, I am."

"I'm Reverend Wilson." He extended his hand to shake Lexi's. "I've heard a great deal about you from both your grandparents."

Lexi nodded numbly and invited him inside. She was grateful that her mother entered at that moment. Grandma Carson was sleeping but the Reverend didn't seem to mind. He asked if he could speak to Lexi and her mother instead.

"I wanted to express my deep sorrow at the passing of your father and grandfather," the kindly pastor said. "I'm sure you know how deep Fred's faith was. He knew that when he left this world, he'd be with our Heavenly Father."

Lexi couldn't move. Her body seemed made of stone as she sat on the couch, listening to the pastor talk about how familiar Christ was with suffering.

Lexi peeked at her mother out of the corner of her eye. Her mother was silently listening to everything the pastor said, a gentle smile forming on her lips.

Lexi wished she could get some comfort from this man's words. She felt numb. It was as though her heart had been replaced by a stone. In a way, the numbness was a relief. She didn't feel anything. Not anger or guilt or sadness. Just emptiness.

After the pastor left, Mrs. Leighton placed her hands on Lexi's shoulders. "Honey, I'm worried about you."

"Don't be; I'll be fine."

"You seem so remote."

"I can't help it. I feel funny inside. It's as if I can't go to God and talk to Him anymore."

Mrs. Leighton looked at her daughter sadly. "It's only a temporary feeling, Lexi. God never leaves us.

He never changes. We can move away from Him, but He never moves away from us."

So that was it, Lexi thought, as she dressed for the family's visit to the funeral home. She'd moved away from God. Could that cause this deep, aching emptiness? She didn't know. Strangely, she didn't care either.

She brushed her hair until her head ached and then walked downstairs to join her family.

On the way to the funeral home, a nervous knot settled in her stomach.

Ben sat poised on the edge of the car's backseat, his little hands folded in his lap, his eyes huge with wonder and curiosity.

As Lexi's parents talked quietly in the front seat, Ben poked Lexi with his finger. "Lexi!"

"What is it, Ben?"

"What's Grandpa going to look like dead?"

"Oh, Ben!" Lexi blurted, then bit her tongue. It was a question he had every right to ask, one she should try to answer. Grandpa Carson was Benjamin's grandfather too. "Kind of like he's sleeping, Ben," Lexi explained.

"If he's sleeping, could he wake up?"

"No, Ben. Not this time. This is a different kind of sleep. A permanent kind. The kind that lasts forever."

Ben's eyes grew wide. "I'm not going to go to sleep tonight. I don't want to go to sleep forever."

"No, Ben, that's not what I meant at all."

"It isn't?" He relaxed.

"M-Maybe you'd better talk to Mother about

this. . . ." Lexi stammered. "I'm not very good at explaining things."

Ben's eyes showed his surprise. "But Lexi knows everything!" he protested.

"Not this time, Sweetheart. Lexi doesn't know everything this time."

At the funeral home, Mrs. Leighton took Lexi and Benjamin aside. "I want you children to know that you can feel free to express your emotions—anything you feel or think. And don't be afraid to cry. Everybody cries at a time like this. Don't try to hold it inside."

While she was talking, Ben pulled on her coat sleeve. "What is it, Ben?"

"Let's go see Grandpa now. I want to see Grandpa dead."

Lexi turned white. "Why did he say that?" she hissed.

Mrs. Leighton shook her head. "Don't be angry with him, Lexi. Children aren't afraid of things unless adults teach them to be. Ben is curious. He loved his grandfather. He has no fear of his body. All those fears are learned from adults who don't want to face death."

"How can you be so calm, Mom?"

Mrs. Leighton's eyes misted. "I'm not calm, Lexi, not really. I'm trying to be strong for you and for your grandmother and for Ben. Besides that, I know Grandpa's in heaven. He's happy. That's very comforting to me. And I want to act as natural as possible for Ben's sake. It's especially difficult for him to understand. Actually, it's not so frightening as it might seem."

"It's frightening to me," Lexi said grudgingly. "I don't even understand why we're here."

"It's best that we take this opportunity to say goodbye, Lexi," Mrs. Leighton explained. "Remember when Ben's friend lost his pet? In a situation like that, there are two things parents can do. They can either remove the pet quickly and pretend the death didn't happen—they might even go right out and buy a new pet for the child. Or, they can give the child time to grieve and to mourn before they get a substitute pet.

"People we love aren't quickly replaced, Lexi. We need time to feel sad. Then after a while we'll begin to remember the good things that we shared with Grandpa.

"Pretty soon, though we loved him and will miss him, we'll be able to go on with our lives. Tonight, and tomorrow at the funeral, are our chances to say goodbye. We'll be with friends and family and people who love us. It's okay if you don't like it, Lexi. It's okay to be unhappy. I'm terribly unhappy, too."

"But you're so . . ." Lexi struggled for the right word, "so strong."

"Not on my own, Lexi. God's helping me. Ask Him to help you too."

Lexi didn't want to admit to her mother that she hadn't been talking to God much lately. When she had talked to Him, she'd been very angry. She still didn't understand why He'd let this happen to her. Everything she'd ever learned or thought or believed about God had flown out the window with Grandpa's death.

The pastor who'd come to the door yesterday was

at the funeral home. He was having a serious conversation with Jim Leighton when Lexi walked into the room. He greeted Lexi and her mother with a gentle smile.

"I was just sharing a verse with Mr. Leighton that might be of help and comfort to you at this time."

Lexi looked at the man doubtfully. What could comfort her? Nothing.

"Let not your hearts be troubled: believe in God, believe also in me. In my Father's house are many rooms; if it were not so, would I have told you that I go to prepare a place for you? And when I go and prepare a place for you, I will come again and will take you to myself, that where I am you may be also."

Lexi listened, trying to imagine what God's house might look like.

———

On the way back from the funeral home, Ben sat serenely in the backseat, humming to himself. There were no tears in his eyes. Lexi stared at her brother enviously. He really was an example of believing as a little child. He'd been told that Grandpa was in heaven and he believed it.

Lexi longed to be more like Ben. For the first time in her life, she was questioning God's wisdom and the part He played in her life. It frightened her more than she'd ever been frightened before.

Chapter Seven

It seemed to Lexi that she lay awake all night, and just when she'd fallen asleep the alarm rang. It was time to get up and get ready for the funeral.

Lexi noticed that the church was full of friends as the family took their places in the front row. Why, she wondered, did she feel so strange, as though someone else were using her body, forcing it to walk in stiff, jerky motions through the sad ordeal?

She barely listened to the pastor's sermon until Psalm 23:4 caught her attention.

> Even though I walk through the valley of the shadow of death, I will fear no evil, for you are with me; your rod and your staff, they comfort me.

Is it really true, Lexi wondered, *that God loves us that much? That He truly is with us?* If so, she could cope with anything. Ben and her parents believed that verse. Lexi looked down at her hands folded neatly in her lap. She used to believe it too. Why was she doubting now just when she needed her faith the most?

Lexi glanced at Grandma at the far end of the pew. She looked tiny and pale and helpless in her dark dress and hat. Lexi's mother had fixed Grandma's hair in soft little waves that framed her face. She looked sweet and ageless.

A rush of sadness filled Lexi again. Grandpa's place was next to Grandma. Grandma shouldn't have to be all alone.

Grandma was acting like someone else was using her body, too. Maybe she felt as Lexi did, like a puppet being jerked through the motions of these horrible days. It was like being a stranger in your own body.

Suddenly Lexi realized that the pastor had invited the people from the congregation to join their family for lunch in the basement after the service. She drew in a sharp breath. The hard part was over. Now all she had to do was face a sea of strangers. Then she could go home to relax and shed the tears she'd been holding inside.

In the basement of the church, Mr. and Mrs. Leighton sat with Grandma at a table. "Would you like some lunch, Mom? A cup of coffee, a sandwich?"

Grandma shook her head. "Oh, my no, I'm too full to eat," she said, sounding bright and carefree, not at all like Lexi expected she would sound after coming from her husband's funeral. "Besides, I have to watch my waist. I wouldn't want to get too fat, you know."

"You don't have to worry about that." Mrs. Leighton wore a puzzled frown. She didn't understand Grandma's behavior either. "Why don't I just bring you some food. You can eat what you want."

Grandma Carson didn't say yes or no. Her attention wandered to one of the light fixtures in the ceiling.

When Lexi and her parents returned carrying plates of food, Grandmother was sitting at the table smiling and humming.

"Her shoes!" Lexi gasped.

They all stared at the place setting before Grandma. The knife and spoon were at the right, with the cup and saucer above the knife. The fork was on the left, and sitting conspicuously where her plate should go, Grandmother's shoes were on the table!

"Mom, your shoes," Marilyn Leighton sounded stunned.

Grandma Carson patted the heels of her shoes. "Yes, aren't they pretty? They're new."

"But you mustn't put your shoes on the table, Mom."

"Why not? The table wasn't very pretty without them."

Lexi stared at her grandmother in shock.

"Why don't we put your shoes on the floor, and this plate of food in front of you," Mr. Leighton spoke softly.

Grandma shook her head adamantly. "Oh, no. My feet hurt. I don't want my shoes on the floor. I want them here on the table where I can look at them."

The basement was starting to fill with guests. In a quick movement, Mrs. Leighton plucked the shoes off the table and placed them on the floor.

"You cannot have your shoes on the table, Mom. Now, try to eat some of this good food."

Just as quickly, Grandma seemed to forget about her shoes, and looked with interest at the plate of food.

Lexi had a cold, sick feeling in the pit of her stomach.

Grandmother floated in and out of the conversations around her like a helium-filled balloon tethered to the earth and swaying in the wind. When friends of the family came to greet her and express their condolences, Grandma didn't seem to know whether to laugh or cry.

Sometimes when someone would make an attempt at light-heartedness, she would burst into tears. Then when someone nearly sobbing came to grasp her hand, she would cackle with glee.

By the time the last guest had left, Lexi felt like she'd been stretched and pulled and tugged in every direction.

She sighed in relief when her father announced that it was time to return to her grandmother's house. At least if Grandmother were going to do strange things, it would be in the privacy of her own home, not in public where everyone would wonder what was wrong with her.

The incident with Grandma and her shoes was the first of many odd occurrences.

"Everybody come to supper now," Grandma announced brightly, as she walked into the living room where Lexi and her parents were playing a board game with Ben.

"Mom, did you fix supper already?" Marilyn Leighton jumped to her feet. "I could have helped you."

"It was nothing, dear," Grandma Carson said

with a flutter of her hand. "I just popped one of those casseroles into the oven and cut some of the cake that Jenny Olson brought over. It's her special pound cake. It's Fred's favorite, you know. Come. Come to dinner." Grandma flapped her apron and shooed them toward the kitchen.

Lexi trailed after her mother and father, bumping into her father's back as he jerked to a halt in the kitchen doorway. "Dad, what's wrong?"

"Shhh, Lexi," he said, holding up a hand.

Lexi peered around her father's shoulder. Every light in the kitchen was on. Half the dishes in the cupboard were sitting on the counter, each with a tiny piece of pound cake. The table was set with dirty dishes from the dishwasher.

"Come, come. Sit down and eat. It's almost ready." Grandma bustled at the stove and opened the oven door. "Oh, my. What's gone wrong? The oven is broken. There's no heat in here." She fussed over the cold casserole. "Jim, we're going to have to call the repairmen. There's no heat in here."

"I think you forgot to turn the oven on," Jim Leighton said gently.

"Mother, where did you get these dishes?" Marilyn pointed to the table.

"From the dishwasher, why?"

"They aren't clean."

"They aren't?" Grandma Carson peered at the table as if she were seeing it for the first time. "Why, they aren't, are they." A look of confusion passed over her face. "Now, why on earth did I do that?"

Hurriedly, Mrs. Leighton gathered the dishes. "It's okay, Mom. You had your mind on other things.

By the time I get these dishes washed and the table reset, that casserole will be hot. Turn on the oven, Jim."

Lexi noticed how shaken her mother was, but felt helpless to do anything about it. Perhaps Grandma was still too upset by the funeral to do things by herself. Lexi didn't even want to consider what had made Grandma put her shoes in the middle of the table at the church.

———

They had just finished eating supper and clearing away the dishes when the door bell rang. It was Hank and June Clausin, Grandma's next-door neighbors.

"We thought we'd come over and see you tonight, Grace. How are you doing?"

Grandma Carson looked at them vaguely. For a brief moment Lexi wondered if she even recognized them. Then her eyes brightened. "Oh my, that was nice of you, but isn't it awfully late?"

Hank looked at his watch. "Well, I don't believe so. It's only seven o'clock."

"Seven o'clock! Oh, my." Grandmother jumped from her chair and put her hands to her cheeks. "Seven o'clock. I should have been in bed hours ago." She patted Hank on the hand and smiled at his wife. "You're dears to come. You can visit with Marilyn and her family, but I really must be in bed." With that, Grandma scurried out of the living room and mounted the stairs to her own bedroom.

Marilyn, with an apologetic look, followed her. She came down a few moments later shaking her head. "I can't change her mind. She thinks it's time to go to bed. I'm so sorry."

Hank shook his head. "Don't worry about it. We're used to it."

"Used to it?" Jim Leighton echoed. "She often behaves like this?"

"She's been getting more and more confused these past few months," Hank admitted. "We worried about her being over here, but Fred always seemed to know just the right thing to say to put her back on track. Once, however, she went to bed at four o'clock in the afternoon and even Fred couldn't figure out how to get her up again."

Marilyn Leighton frowned. "I don't like the way she's behaving. It makes it doubly serious to hear that she was acting confused *before* my father passed away."

Mrs. Leighton glanced at Lexi and then at Ben. "Lexi, will you take your brother into the kitchen and help him do a puzzle? I brought some old ones down from the attic."

Lexi realized her parents wanted to talk privately. "Come on, Ben. Let's do one of Mom's old puzzles." She grabbed him by the hand and they moved into the kitchen. As they worked on the puzzle, the adult voices became a muted drone. Lexi forgot for a few minutes what had been going on in her life. The kitchen was cozy and warm. The puzzle, though old, was fun to do and somewhat distracting.

"Isn't it beautiful, Lexi?" Ben said when they were finished. They both gazed at their accomplishment. It was a picture of flower beds full of roses and a quaint, stone house.

"It is Ben. It's really beautiful."

Ben jumped to his feet. "Then let's go get Grandpa and show him—" Ben stopped mid-sentence. His little jaw dropped and his eyes grew wide.

"It's okay, Ben. It's hard to remember that Grandpa's not here anymore." Lexi forgot her own grief while soothing her little brother.

After they'd broken up the puzzle and put it away, she took him to bed and tucked him in. Long afterward, she could hear the adults downstairs in their prolonged conversation.

———

"Are we going back to Cedar River today?" Lexi asked eagerly. "I can hardly wait to get back to my friends."

"We'll be leaving in three hours, Lexi. Get your suitcase packed and help Ben with his. But first, I need to talk to you." Her father looked serious.

"Yes, Dad? What about?"

"Your mother and I made a decision last night, Lexi."

"What kind of a decision?"

"We're going to take Grandma back to Cedar River with us. She's not well. She shouldn't be left alone. She's very forgetful and disoriented. We'd like to make sure she's all right before we leave her alone in this big old house."

Lexi's mind spun with an array of conflicting emotions. If her parents had announced two weeks ago that they were bringing Grandpa and Grandma to live with them, Lexi would have shouted for joy.

Now, when only Grandmother would be coming, Lexi was dismayed.

She didn't want Grandma to come with them to Cedar River. What if any of her friends saw her Grandmother acting this way?

Chapter Eight

It felt wonderful to be back home! Lexi hurried toward Cedar River High School. Binky and Egg McNaughton were standing in the doorway waiting for her.

"There she is! Welcome back! We missed you Lexi."

Lexi threw her arms around Binky and Egg. "And I missed you guys. It feels wonderful to be here. It feels normal." It was a relief to return to a routine with which she was familiar.

"I've been taking notes for you all week," Binky said proudly. "In every class we share. You can copy them. It should be really easy for you to catch up."

"Except for the tests," Egg said sourly. "Boy, did we have tests this week. We had a test about Teddy Roosevelt that asked questions that Teddy himself couldn't have answered!" Egg began muttering under his breath.

"Don't pay any attention to Egg," Binky told Lexi. "He's been a real grump because he didn't do as well as I did on the test."

"You're a better guesser, that's all," Egg retorted.

Binky made a face and stuck her tongue out at

her brother. Lexi burst out laughing. "It is *so good* to see you two. Just keep on fighting. I love it."

"Not only did I take notes in class," Binky continued, "but I wrote down all the juicy gossip from the whole week. You'll be able to step right in like you were never gone."

Lexi laughed, her eyes shining. "Thanks, you guys. I really needed this. I missed you so much."

"How about me? Did you miss me?" Todd appeared out of nowhere and picked her up in his arms and swung her around.

Lexi threw back her head and laughed. "I missed you most of all."

"More than me?" Egg piped. "Just because he's your boyfriend and looks like a movie star, you think he's somebody special. Hmmmph." Egg complained with a grin.

With Todd's arm still around her, Lexi closed her eyes. She could have stayed there forever. He was so strong and wonderful, and being with him felt so absolutely right. "You smell great. Do you know that?"

Todd blinked in surprise. "I do? Must be my brother Mike's shaving lotion."

"I don't know. Whatever it is, I love it. For the last week, I've been living in a house that smells of dust and cinnamon and flowers." Lexi was very glad to be back.

As Todd, Binky and Egg chattered together, Lexi studied her friends. Their faces looked so beautiful and familiar to her that she felt like crying. If only she could erase the past week from her life! Then everything would be perfect.

Perhaps life would be better now that she was home again with her friends in Cedar River, Lexi mused. Maybe the emotional roller coaster ride she'd been on would come to an end. She could get her mind straightened out here. For the first time in many days, Lexi felt a budding ray of hope.

"Warning bell," Egg yelped. "We'd better hurry or we're going to be late for class."

Todd placed a kiss on the tip of Lexi's nose before they all scattered for their morning classes.

Unfortunately, Mr. Raddis had chosen this day to be particularly boring in history class. As he droned on, Lexi's mind began to wander. She recalled breakfast that morning.

It had been wonderful to see Grandmother standing at the stove in her bathrobe, cooking eggs. Lexi was relieved to see her Grandma acting more like her old self.

"This is good, Grandma," Ben said as he spooned the hot breakfast into his mouth.

Lexi nodded. "Super. I'd forgotten what a good cook you were."

Grandma Carson beamed at the compliment. Lexi noted her mother and father exchanging relieved glances. Perhaps now that Grandma was here, away from the reminders of her sadness, she would return to normal. Lexi ate her breakfast contentedly.

"Aren't you going to eat, Mother?" Mrs. Leighton asked. "You've barely put a bite into your mouth."

"No, no. I don't think so," Grandma said. "I'm not very hungry this morning." She looked down at the bathrobe she was wearing. "In fact, I think I'll go upstairs and get dressed."

"Go ahead. The kids and I will clean up the dishes." Marilyn smiled at her mother. "It's good to have you with us, Mom."

"Yes, yes. I suppose it is," Grandma said vaguely, as if she were answering a statement her daughter hadn't made. "I'll be down when I'm finished dressing." She shuffled slowly toward the door. Lexi could hear each step creak as she mounted the stairs to the second floor.

"She's better this morning, isn't she?" Lexi said hopefully.

"It seems so," Mrs. Leighton said. "It's good to see her keeping busy. I think that's the best thing for Grandma right now."

"You kids can help us with that," Mr. Leighton said. "Bring your friends over to visit. Spend time playing games with Grandma. Let her know that she's welcome here and that she's loved."

"Grandma can play with my toys anytime she wants," Ben announced proudly. "Even the trucks and the puzzles."

"That's very nice of you, Ben," Mrs. Leighton said with a wide smile. "You're a very generous boy."

"Ben is generous," he echoed and laid down his spoon.

For the first time in several days, Lexi felt lightness in her heart. The time for sadness was over. Now they could go on with their lives.

"It seems like Mother is taking an awfully long time to get dressed." Mrs. Leighton fretted as they washed the breakfast dishes and put them away.

"You know women." Mr. Leighton chuckled. "She's probably primping in front of the mirror."

Just then, they heard Grandma coming down the stairs. Her slippered feet shuffled along the floor toward the kitchen.

"There you are, Mom. I was beginning to worry. . . ." The words seemed to catch in her throat.

Lexi turned to see her grandmother enter the kitchen.

She was dressed nicely in a pair of lavender slacks and a lavender blouse. Her hair was neatly combed and she was even wearing a bit of lipstick. But, to Lexi's horror, her grandmother was wearing all of her underwear on the outside of her clothes.

"Grandma!" Ben blurted, his eyes round with amazement. "You've got it backwards!"

Grandma looked down at herself, as if nothing was out of the ordinary. "What's backwards, Benny dear?"

The dish Marilyn Leighton was holding slipped from her hand and clattered to the table.

With lightning speed, she rushed to her mother's side, put one hand on her shoulder and steered her out of the room.

"Come upstairs, Mom. I'll help you dress. I think you're a little mixed up this morning. We'll get things straightened out right away."

Lexi felt as stunned as if she'd been hit in the face. Her stomach churned and whirled. She was afraid she was going to lose the breakfast she had just eaten.

Ben stared through the kitchen door at his mother and his grandmother making their way toward the stairs. "Why did she do that?" Ben asked innocently. "Grandma's funny!"

Mr. Leighton shook his head. "I don't know, Ben. I can't answer that question."

"I don't wear my underwear outside my clothes." Ben looked down at his navy trousers and blue T-shirt. He tugged at his waistband. "They belong under my pants—not on top!" he said with a giggle.

"You're absolutely right, Ben. Grandma must have gotten mixed up this morning."

"Why?" Ben asked again, "What's wrong with Grandma?"

———

Two hours later as Lexi sat in class, she could still hear Ben's question echoing in her mind. *What's wrong with Grandma?* An iciness gripped Lexi's heart.

She knew that her parents had been worrying for some time about Grandma's forgetfulness. She was apt to put something on the stove and leave the burner on high long after she'd taken the pan away. Sometimes after ironing she'd forget to turn off the iron, and occasionally she'd fill the washing machine and then forget to add the soap and the clothes.

They'd all joked about it, but Grandpa had always been there to watch after her.

Now, with Grandpa gone, Grandma's confusion and forgetfulness seemed so much worse. Anyone could be confused and forget something once in a while, Lexi mused, but how could anyone forget that their underwear goes *beneath* their outer clothes? Lexi couldn't understand.

What's wrong with Grandma?

The whole school day had been wasted, Lexi decided after the last bell. She couldn't get her mind off her grandmother. She could barely remember anything the teachers said in class. Standing forlornly at her locker, she was exchanging her books when Jennifer and Binky came up beside her.

"Hi, Lexi. I've hardly seen you all day," Jennifer said.

"I tried to catch you after class but you floated off too quickly," Binky complained. "Have you finished your English assignment yet?"

Lexi shook her head. "I haven't even started it."

"Should we do it together?" Binky asked. "The teacher said it was okay to work in groups."

"That sounds like a good idea." Maybe with her friends to help her, she could keep her mind on her work instead of having it drift to her problems at home.

"Can we go to your place?" Binky asked hopefully. "If we go to mine, Egg will be there pestering us and we'll never get anything done." Her nose wrinkled in distaste. "You know how Egg is."

Normally, Lexi would be happy to have her friends come to her house. Things were different now. She remembered her grandmother again, standing pitifully in the kitchen in her underwear.

But that wasn't going to happen again, Lexi told herself. That was a bizarre, one-time thing. Surely Grandma would be fine this afternoon. "Sure, why not? You can come to my place. My grandmother is staying with us for a while."

"Oh, good," Binky said with genuine excitement in her voice. "You've talked about her so much that I'm anxious to meet her."

Lexi pulled her English books from her locker. "Let's go then. We'd better get started if we're going to get this project done by suppertime."

"You girls need a ride?" Todd called from his '49 Ford Coupe. He and Harry Cramer were moving slowly near the sidewalk where the three girls walked.

Lexi shook her head. "No thanks. It's a beautiful day and we're not far from home."

"Harry and I are on our way to my brother Mike's garage," Todd explained over the car's engine. "The old car is making a strange sound. I'm going to check it out." Todd patted the dashboard. "She's getting to be an old lady, you know. See you girls later." With that, he revved the motor and the boys drove away.

Binky stared after the car with a dreamy expression on her face. "That Todd Winston is such a sweetheart, Lexi. You're so lucky to have him for a boyfriend."

"Well, Harry Cramer isn't bad either, you know."

"True, but there's something really special about Todd. He's so mature and understanding."

"Sounds like you'd better hang on to Todd for dear life," Jennifer warned. "Binky might just break up with Harry to get her hands on Todd."

"Not a chance!" Binky smiled smugly. "Lexi and I have an agreement."

"But Harry's going to graduate," Jennifer pointed out matter-of-factly.

Binky wrinkled her nose. "I know. I hate to think about it. But we'll still be friends. I'm too young to settle down anyway."

"Smart thinking," Lexi agreed. "We're all too

young for that. But Todd is a special guy, alright."

Their conversation brought them to the front steps of the Leighton home. The girls walked inside and looked around. Lexi's mom was in the kitchen kneading bread.

Lexi's gaze darted from one room to the other. "Your grandmother's taking a nap, Lexi," her mother said.

"Oh, okay." Lexi felt a sense of relief wash over her. Grandma made her nervous. No one ever knew what was going to happen next. Perhaps it was a good thing that she was napping. The tension that Lexi had felt began to melt away.

The three girls scanned the cupboards and came up with a bag of chips and a large bottle of cola.

"Okay if we take this to my room, Mom?" Lexi asked.

"How about something more healthy? There're carrot sticks, celery and cauliflower in the fridge."

Jennifer, Binky and Lexi all shook their heads in unison. "That stuff is *too* good for us. What we really need right now is junk food."

Mrs. Leighton pursed her lips. "Well, there will be plenty of carrots for supper."

In Lexi's room, the threesome spread their English books and papers across the bed and began to work. It was nearly six o'clock by the time they finished their project and gathered up their things.

"I'd better get going," Binky said. "I'm going to be late for supper."

"Yeah, then you might have to eat here," Jennifer pointed out. "And you'd have to eat carrots. Lots of them."

The three girls laughed as they clattered down the stairs. Lexi glanced into the living room and noticed her grandmother standing in front of the fireplace. She looked very pretty. Her white hair was arranged in soft curls, and she wore a crisp, flower-print cotton dress. Lexi thought she looked just like a grandmother should look—soft, sweet and gentle.

But something was wrong. Just as Lexi would have greeted her and introduced her friends, Grandmother began talking to herself in the large mirror that hung over the fireplace. She waved her finger at the image and scolded, "Now shame on you. You mustn't do that anymore. You're being a very naughty girl." Her voice rose to a near shout. "Stop that! Start behaving yourself right this instant!"

Lexi felt a burning sensation from the top of her head to her toes. She flushed a deep crimson. Grabbing her friends by the elbows, she steered them toward the front door.

"Don't pay any attention to Grandma," she said. "She does funny things sometimes."

"Who is she scolding?" Binky wondered, her face as curious as Ben's had been this morning.

"I don't know. Herself, Mom, me. I really don't know." Lexi shook her head. She pushed her friends out the door and onto the porch. "Thanks for coming over. I feel much better now that I have all my English done," Lexi babbled nervously.

Binky and Jennifer descended the steps and were on their way. It was obvious Lexi didn't want to discuss her grandmother's problems.

Lexi scampered inside and shut the door, leaning against it heavily. Her legs trembled until she was afraid they might not hold her. First her underwear on the outside of her clothes. Now this!

"Lexi? Is something wrong?" Marilyn Leighton came from the kitchen wiping her hands on her apron.

"It's Grandma," Lexi pointed weakly toward the living room.

She had stopped scolding her image in the mirror, but was whimpering pitifully, and Mrs. Leighton soothed her in a soft, kind voice, "It's okay, Mom. Come with me." Lexi's mother guided Grandma Carson toward the stairs, speaking gently to her. "It's okay, Mom. You just had a little accident. It's no problem. I'll help you get cleaned up."

Lexi stared after them. Her jaw dropped in amazement when she realized what had happened. Her grandmother had wet her pants.

Lexi leaned her forehead against the cool, hard wood of the door jamb and closed her eyes. "Oh no," she murmured. The image of Jennifer and Binky staring at her grandmother came into Lexi's mind.

She raised her head and lifted her jaw in grim determination. It was never going to happen again, Lexi vowed. Never. She would make sure of that. She would never again invite her friends to her home as long as Grandmother lived with them.

Never, never, never.

Chapter Nine

"I hope no one else gets this awful flu that's going around," Mrs. Leighton said. She distractedly pulled her fingers through her hair. "Ben feels just terrible."

"What did the doctor say about him?" Lexi asked.

Mrs. Leighton shook her head. "That's the odd part. He said that Ben should be getting over this more quickly than he is. Usually Ben bounces right back from any sort of bug or cold, and he's so slow to complain. But, this time. . . ." She shook her head helplessly. "He's never behaved like this before."

"Mom—my!" he wailed from the next room.

"Oh, dear, he's awake again. Lexi, would you pour him a glass of juice? I'd better see what he wants."

Lexi couldn't remember ever seeing her mother so tired and haggard-looking. Between Ben's crying and whining and Grandmother's strange antics, Mrs. Leighton was busy every moment of the day.

Lexi brought the juice into the living room where her little brother was wrapped in a blanket like a little papoose. His dark silky hair was spiked across the pillow. His nose was red, his eyes were pink, and he was sucking his thumb—something he hadn't done for years.

"Are you still feeling sick, Ben?" Lexi asked sympathetically. "Maybe this juice will help."

"Play with me, Lexi?" he murmured pitifully.

Lexi sighed. She'd done nothing but play with Ben all day Saturday and ever since she'd returned from church this morning. She'd read him books. They'd put together puzzles. She'd rubbed his back. Every time she stopped, he'd clutch at her hand and beg for more.

Ben reached out and grabbed his mother's sleeve. "Stay with me, Mommy," he pleaded.

"Ben, I have to cook dinner now."

"Ben's not hungry," he pouted. A single tear rolled down his cheek.

"No, maybe you aren't hungry, but your daddy is, I'm sure. Lexi will stay with you."

With that, another tear fell, and soon Ben began to sob. Mrs. Leighton looked wearily at Lexi.

Just then, Mr. Leighton appeared at the living room door. "What's going on here?" Ben was writhing and wailing on the couch as though he were in agony.

"I don't know what to do for this child anymore, Jim. The doctor said he should be well enough to go to school tomorrow. But, look at him."

Ben moaned and struggled on the couch.

"Maybe you should take him back to the doctor. Maybe there's something else wrong that he didn't catch the first time."

At that, Ben began a pitiful, high-pitched squeal that seared Lexi's heart.

"Don't do that, Ben. You're all right. You'll be just fine." She kneeled down on the floor next to the couch and took him in her arms. "You're okay, Ben. You're going to be okay."

As she held her trembling little brother, a thought came into her mind. She laid him back against the pillow and took his face in her hands. She looked deep into his eyes. "Ben. Ben."

He snuffled and wiggled, but she wouldn't let go.

"Look at me, Ben, and listen to me. Are you *afraid* of being sick?"

"Don't like it. Don't like it," he fussed.

"Listen, Ben," Lexi said firmly. "The last person who got sick in our family was Grandpa, wasn't it."

Ben nodded his head forlornly, and the tears began to well up again.

"But you're not sick like Grandpa."

Ben held still for a moment. "I'm not?"

Lexi's mother knelt beside her and she ran a gentle hand across Ben's forehead. "Ben, have you been worrying that what happened to Grandpa is going to happen to you?"

Ben nodded solemnly.

Lexi held Ben's hands in her own. "Grandpa had a stroke, Ben. That's something that happens to older people. Not little children. You have the flu. You're not going to die. The doctor says you're going to get better. In fact, he thinks you'll be able to go back to the Academy tomorrow."

Ben sniffled and looked doubtfully at Lexi. Then he turned trusting eyes to his mother.

Mrs. Leighton nodded. Her eyes were bright with tears. "Oh, Ben, I'm so sorry. I didn't realize you were more scared than sick! Have you been worrying all weekend about this?"

Ben's face crumpled. Lexi got up to allow her mother to cradle Ben on her lap.

"Benjamin, it hasn't been the flu that's been making you feel so sick today and yesterday. It's all that worrying you've been doing."

Ben blinked his eyes and asked, "Ben's going to get better now?"

"Of course he is. Ben was getting better all along. He just scared himself." Mrs. Leighton looked at him sternly. "And from now on, when you have worries like that don't keep them inside. Come to me or Daddy or Lexi and tell us about it. Even if it's something that's very hard for you to explain. You can talk to us about anything, Ben. Do you know that?"

Ben nodded mutely, then buried his face in his mother's shoulder. His body trembled as he sighed with relief.

"Jim, why don't you take Ben upstairs and put him in the bathtub? He's all hot and sweaty from crying. I think he's going to feel much better now."

Ben reached for his father. Mr. Leighton carried him gently up the stairs. After they left the room, Mrs. Leighton turned to her daughter. "Thank you, Lexi. That was a very wise conclusion."

Lexi shrugged, "Not so wise, really. All of a sudden I just realized that Ben might be thinking of how Grandpa got sick and died."

"I'm surprised I didn't think of it earlier," Mrs. Leighton said. "It's very difficult for children to understand about death. And of course for Ben, it's probably even more difficult. I'm proud of the way you've handled yourself through all of this, Lexi—with both Ben and with Grandma."

Lexi nodded but didn't speak. She was glad she could be of help to her little brother. She was indeed proud of that. She wished she could be proud of the way she felt about her grandmother. But there were times when she wished Grandma hadn't come to live with them.

———

The entire gang had gathered at the Hamburger Shack. Egg and Todd were in the mood for a party.

"My parents are painting the house and it smells awful," Egg announced. "We can't party there."

"And my dad has the flu that's been going around." Jennifer held her nose. "I'm staying away from home as much as possible until he gets over it."

"Well, I can't have any party at my house," Harry said ruefully. "My parents have invited some friends over. My Mom's been vacuuming and dusting for three days. She's been making me tiptoe around so I don't disturb anything. It's crazy. The guests will never notice how much work she's done. She'll only have to clean up again after they leave."

"Don't fight it," Binky said knowingly. "Parents are hard to understand. My mother says I'll start understanding her when I become a parent myself." She made a face. "That means I'll be old before I can figure her out."

Todd turned to Lexi. "How about it? Can you have a party at your house?"

Lexi had been quiet through the entire conversation. Now she shook her head. "I don't think so."

"Oh? I thought Ben was feeling much better."

"He is. He's back at the Academy."

"Well, then there are no flu bugs there."

"I can't guys. I'm really sorry. I'm afraid if we had a party at our house, it would disturb my grandmother."

"I forgot about that," Harry said understandingly. "Sorry."

Binky and Jennifer exchanged knowing glances, remembering how her grandmother had been the last time they'd been at Lexi's house.

Only Todd looked at Lexi curiously.

Anna Marie Arnold, one of Lexi's newer friends, spoke up, "If Lexi can't have the party at her house, why don't we have it at mine?"

"You mean it, Anna Marie? Your folks won't mind?" Lexi asked.

She shook her head. "You know my mother. She loves to cook. I think it would be a great idea to have a party at my place."

"All right!" Egg rubbed his hands together with glee. Then he pulled a pen from his pocket and grabbed a napkin from the dispenser. "I'll be in charge of planning the menu."

"That's rude, Egg," Binky piped. "If it's at Anna Marie's house, she should plan the menu."

Anna Marie shook her head. "That's all right. Whatever you guys want is fine. I'll just tell my mom."

"See." Egg made a face at Binky who stuck her tongue out.

"We'll have a vegetable tray, a fruit tray, and a bunch of crackers," Egg announced as he scribbled on the napkin. Egg still maintained some of his health-kick habits from weeks on a special diet. At least he didn't want tofu and bean sprouts.

"No way," Binky moaned. "We'll have chips and hot sauce, and sodas and brownies!"

Egg shook his head. "Too much sugar and caffeine!"

"Well, the other stuff's too boring and healthy," Binky protested.

Jennifer rolled her eyes. "While you two are fighting over the menu, the rest of us should plan the party. I'd like to watch a video."

Harry nodded. "That sounds good. And games— anybody got any good games?"

While the others chattered about the party, Todd turned again to Lexi. "Maybe you were smart telling them not to come to your house. I don't know if I'd want this crew storming through mine, either."

"It's not that, Todd," Lexi admitted. "It's just too hard right now."

Todd's expression was serious. "You never seem to want anyone to come to your house anymore. I can't remember the last time you invited me inside."

"That's not true," she protested. Even as she said it, Lexi knew he was right.

Todd ignored her comment. "Why don't you want anyone to come in anymore, Lexi?"

"Grandma needs to be quiet," Lexi said, covering the real truth. "She's got this schedule she has to maintain. Eating at a certain time, sleeping at a certain time; you know how old people are."

"I don't know a lot of old people like that."

"Well, that's how my grandma is!" Lexi said emphatically. "Don't you believe me?"

"There's no reason to get upset," Todd said quietly. "We aren't coming to your house."

"Well, it's not because of me," Lexi said defensively. "It's because of Grandma. You guys have to understand that."

Todd gave her a pitying look.

Lexi was silent then, her head down, staring at the floor, willing herself not to cry. This was so embarrassing! This business with her grandmother had gotten out of hand.

Lexi had never been ashamed of anyone in her family before. Even Ben's condition had never embarrassed her. But her grandmother was doing odd things every day when the family least expected them.

They'd be having a wonderful conversation at the dinner table and suddenly Grandma would pick up a dish and throw it across the room. Once, when Lexi was coming up the stairs to talk to her mother, she heard her grandmother swearing—something she'd never done before.

In fact, she'd never said a bad word in her life. She was shocked by anyone who did. And there she was, standing in her bedroom, saying all these horrible words! It just didn't make sense.

What if Grandmother did something like that while one of her friends was there? Lexi felt a sick, tight feeling inside. She hated to be secretive. It was unlike her to keep things from her friends, but lately she'd kept a lot to herself. The more strange things Lexi saw her grandmother do, the less Lexi felt like talking about it.

"Sounds like we've got the party all planned," Egg spoke up, jolting Lexi from her thoughts. She realized she hadn't even heard them making their plans.

As everyone began to go their separate ways, Todd stopped Lexi. "Can I take you home?"

"Thanks, I'd appreciate it."

Once they were in the car, Todd gave her a worried glance. "Are you sure you're all right, Lexi?"

"Oh, sure, I'm fine," she lied. "Why?"

"You were so quiet today."

"I guess I didn't have much to say."

Todd's mouth was set firmly. "You haven't had a lot to say for quite a while, Lexi. Ever since your grandfather died."

Lexi looked down at the floorboards of the old car. Todd always knew and understood what was going on with her. He could figure her out more quickly than anyone else.

"It's—it's just all so sad," she stammered. "I can't explain it."

They pulled up in front of the Leighton house. Todd draped his arm over the back of the seat and fingered Lexi's hair. "You can talk to me about it, Lexi. I'm always ready to listen."

A movement at the large front window of the house drew their attention. Lexi's grandmother stood with her face pressed against the glass, staring out at them. Her shoulders twitched and she looked like a bewildered child framed in the window.

Please, Grandma, Lexi pleaded silently. *Don't embarrass me like this.*

"Lexi, what's the matter?"

Lexi turned sharply toward him. "Everything's fine, Todd. Why don't you believe me?"

"Well, I was just thinking—" He glanced toward the picture window again, but Lexi's grandmother had moved away.

"Maybe you'd better not think so hard, Todd. And don't worry about me. I'm fine. *Understand?*" Lexi surprised herself. She had never used such a tone of voice with Todd before. But she didn't want him to ask any more questions. She didn't know how to answer him, or how to explain to him or anyone else about her grandmother.

She wished the whole situation would just go away, that things would return to normal. But as long as Grandmother lived with them, she would have to live with the dread of what would happen next.

Lexi opened the car door with a jerk. "Thanks for the ride, Todd."

"Lexi?" Todd's voice sounded hurt, confused.

"I have a lot of work to do tonight, Todd. I really can't sit here any longer and talk to you."

"All right," he said, bewildered.

Lexi slammed the door and hurried up the sidewalk to the house. Once inside, she closed the door and leaned against it. Her knees were shaking, her pulse pounded in her temples and her stomach felt tied in knots.

Oh, Todd, what have I done? Now I've hurt you too!

She longed to run outside again, to apologize to him, but Grandmother sat in her rocker, singing that old lullaby and rocking her imaginary baby. She couldn't let him see her grandma like this.

No matter how much she wanted to explain what was happening to her family, she couldn't. She wouldn't. She would keep this nightmare to herself.

Chapter Ten

Late the next afternoon when Lexi arrived home, her parents were waiting for her in the living room.

"Lexi?" Mr. Leighton said. "Come in here, dear. We'd like to talk to you."

Lexi felt fluttery inside. *Now what? More trouble*, she supposed. Everything in her life was trouble lately.

"What is it?" Lexi flung herself into an easy chair across from her parents.

"It's about your grandmother."

Lexi's spine became rigid. "Grandma? Has something happened to her?"

"No, no, she's upstairs resting," Mrs. Leighton assured her.

"Oh." Lexi slouched against the chair again. As angry as she was at her grandmother's odd behavior, she didn't want anything to happen to her.

Her mother's eyes looked sad and tired. "Your father and I took your grandmother to the clinic today."

"Really?" Lexi's heart pounded in her throat. "What's wrong?"

"There are more tests to be done, but the doctors

think your grandmother is suffering from Alzheimer's disease."

Alzheimer's. What a strange-sounding disease. "What's that?"

Mr. and Mrs. Leighton looked distressed. "I know you've noticed Grandma's strange behavior ever since Grandpa's death."

Lexi nodded.

"Well, all the things she's been doing and saying, the strange way she's been acting, are all part of the disease."

"How can that be?"

"According to the doctor, one of the symptoms of Alzheimer's is memory loss. It can mean a shortened attention span or poor judgment. Sometimes a patient will become disoriented. They might even forget how to speak. Even their personalities may change."

It did sound like what Grandma was going through alright.

"We think Grandma has had Alzheimer's for several years, but your Grandpa was able to 'cover for her' and hide her confusion from us. If she made a bad decision or forgot something, Grandpa helped her out. Neither of us realized how badly she'd declined until Grandpa died. After he was gone, she became extremely confused."

"Is it going to get worse?" Lexi blurted.

Mrs. Leighton nodded sadly. "Unfortunately, it is. The doctor says some of his patients eventually forget how to eat or how to get dressed by themselves."

Lexi was shocked. "Can't they do something? Give her something? A pill? Can't she have surgery?

There must be some way to fix this!"

"Alzheimer's is a disease of the brain, Lexi. There is very little doctors can do. Changes in a person's behavior are inevitable."

"But Grandma looks all right," Lexi protested. "She doesn't *look* sick."

"Well, people with the disease do often appear perfectly healthy, while they really are quite ill. One of Grandma's doctor's patients was able to go jogging and play racquetball, but couldn't remember how to dial the telephone."

"You mean she's going to stay this way? Or get worse?" Lexi thought about all the painful days they'd spent coaxing her grandmother out of her odd behavior.

Mrs. Leighton pulled a sheet of paper from her purse. "The doctor gave me a list of symptoms, Lexi. Your father and I felt that you should know what kinds of things might happen."

Lexi could see the pain in her mother's eyes.

"It's not uncommon for people with the disease to lose their way in familiar rooms or forget how to turn on the radio or television. If Grandma seems confused, you'll just have to help her, Lexi. And don't be hurt if she forgets your name. It's all because of the disease. She can't help it."

Mrs. Leighton covered her face with her hands, and her shoulders trembled. "I can't believe this is happening to Mom."

"The bank called today, too," Mr. Leighton said soberly. "Grandmother can't take care of herself anymore."

"Why? What do you mean?" Lexi asked, trying to

make sense of all this information. She was beginning to panic.

"It seems that she hasn't paid any bills for a long time. She must have also ignored the warning notices. I'm going to Oxford City tomorrow to try to straighten things out." Mr. Leighton shook his head. "I suppose she was too sick to tell Grandpa that the bills weren't being paid. She'd always taken care of them for the family."

"What are we going to do?" Lexi asked.

"There's not much we can do, Lexi. There is no cure for the condition. We think we only have one option."

"What's that?" Lexi was almost afraid to ask. She was hoping against hope that there was a way to change this horrible situation.

"For right now, we're going to keep Grandmother here with us. She can't go back home to Oxford City. That's pretty obvious. In her good moments, she's still a very independent lady, and she'd fight going to a nursing home. And we do think it's important for her to feel the love of her family right now. That may be the one thing that will get through to her, the knowledge that she's loved and cared for."

Her grandmother would never be well. She would never return from this darkness she was wandering in or the confusion that dominated her mind. Lexi didn't try to hold back the tears that coursed down her cheeks. This was the most awful news she had ever heard. Even more awful than her grandfather's death.

Grandpa wouldn't suffer anymore. Poor Grandma would continue to walk aimlessly around making odd sounds and shouting at herself in the mirror, or putting her clothes on backwards. The thought broke Lexi's heart.

Still another emotion tugged at Lexi's heart. It was guilt.

"Does she have to stay with us? Is it really the best place for her?" Lexi hated herself for asking these questions.

"We think so. At least for the time being," Lexi's mother said. "We'll put her on a routine that she can remember and love her as much as we can."

"I don't think I can bear to see this happening to her," Lexi protested. "It's too awful."

Lexi realized that what she really meant was, *I don't want my friends to see my grandmother acting this way.* What would they think? What would they say? Would they laugh behind her back?

Lexi remembered how Jennifer and Binky had stared at her grandmother as she shouted to herself in the fireplace mirror. Could she bear to have Egg or Todd, Harry or Anna Marie see that? She didn't think so. It was too awful. Too embarrassing. Too humiliating.

How could Grandma do this to her? A darkness settled over Lexi's spirit, so heavy that it seemed to smother her. How could *God* do this to her?

Lexi stood up. "I think I'd like to go upstairs and be alone for a while."

"Of course, honey," her mother said. "Remember, anytime you want to talk about it, we're here for you."

Lexi nodded numbly. It was a bitter thought to realize that she was ashamed of her own grandmother. She'd handled Ben's disability. Why couldn't she handle this one?

Maybe it was because her grandmother had always been smart, strong, pretty and loving. Grandmothers weren't supposed to be confused, silly-acting and embarrassing.

Lexi wanted to think of her grandmother in the way she did her grandfather—strong and able and caring, not mixed-up and pitiful like she was now.

Why, God? Why? Lexi wanted to raise her fists to the sky and scream. *This is a dirty trick, God. A dirty trick to play on my grandmother and on me.* She trembled with anger, rage and guilt. Flinging herself onto her bed, she buried her face in her pillow and sobbed.

After a long while, she lifted her head from her wet pillow and sat up. She looked at the Bible on the corner of her nightstand, but couldn't pick it up. She'd always turned to the Scriptures when things got too hard to handle. But today, with her grief so strong and the wounds so fresh, she just couldn't.

Two voices struggled within her. One said, "Pick up your Bible. Read. Draw strength from Him." The other, loud and angry, screamed, "God did this to you and to your family! How can you trust Him? How can you count on Him?"

Lexi stared out the window until the light began to fade. She had never felt so hopeless or alone.

"You're with me, aren't you God?" she murmured weakly. "Even though I can't hear You or feel You right now, You promised You'd be with me."

Feeling somewhat comforted, Lexi lay down again, curled up and fell asleep.

———

Even though Lexi knew now what was causing her grandmother's odd behavior, it was still difficult to accept and cope with her condition.

Rather than face her friends at Anna Marie's party, Lexi gave them an excuse for not attending. She went home alone from school, and found her grandmother wandering aimlessly in the front yard. "Grandma?" she called. "Are you looking at the flowers?"

Grandma looked up, her eyes vague. "Who are you?" she asked, a confused expression on her face.

"It's Lexi, Grandma. Lexi. Don't you remember me?"

"I have a granddaughter named Lexi," she said brightly. "She's a pretty girl. You'd like her."

"I *am* Lexi, Grandmother."

"She's a pretty girl. Pretty girl. You'd like her." Grandma meandered through the yard repeating the phrases over and over.

"What are you doing? What are you looking for?" Lexi demanded.

"Where's the kitchen in this house?" Grandma said, her brow furrowed. She was holding an empty coffee cup. "I want a cup of coffee and I can't find the kitchen."

Lexi felt sick to her stomach. "Why don't I show you where the kitchen is," she managed to say gently.

Grandma nodded happily. "Oh, you're a nice girl just like my granddaughter. You'd like her. Why don't you come home with me and meet her?"

Lexi sighed and relented. There was no use trying to change the confusion of Grandma's mind. "All right, I'd like that. I'd like to meet Lexi."

"Oh good. She's such a pretty girl."

Lexi settled her grandmother at the kitchen table with a cup of coffee.

Just then, Lexi's mother walked into the room. "Oh, hi, honey. How was school today?" Mrs. Leighton looked thin. She'd lost several pounds since Grandma came to stay. She looked tired too, as if she weren't getting enough sleep at night.

"I found Grandma outside on the lawn," Lexi said softly.

Mrs. Leighton tensed. "Oh, dear, she could have walked into the street."

"She was looking for the kitchen. She wanted a cup of coffee."

Lexi's mother sank to a stool at the counter. "It's getting worse, Lexi, and it's happening so quickly. This morning she decided to make tea, and left the kettle on till it went dry. I found it just in time. We could have had a fire."

Lexi glanced at the stove. Her mother had removed all the knobs. "They're in the cupboard," her mother explained. "It's much safer that way. Grandmother can't turn on the stove herself."

"What if she finds them?" Lexi was worried.

"I don't think she will, Lexi. It would be a pretty difficult task for her to put them on anyway." Mrs. Leighton smiled faintly. "Yesterday, she asked me all day long how old I was. By the end of the day, I felt twenty years older than I am."

"You're going to get sick yourself, Mom, if you aren't careful," Lexi said. "Are you sure you can take care of her?"

"I have to do this, Lexi. I just have to. When you and Ben were small there were times when you were crying or sick and I thought I would collapse from exhaustion. But I kept going. I had to. And I know my mother did the same thing for me. Now she needs me. I have to care for her."

"Then who will care for us?" Lexi protested.

Angrily, Lexi threw a towel onto the counter and walked out of the room. *Grandma this and Grandma that.* The whole Leighton household revolved around Grandma's every need and wish. Lexi was getting tired of it. And she was afraid that her life was never going to be the same again.

Chapter Eleven

The family walked a daily tightrope, wondering when Grandmother would be clear and when she'd be confused. Fortunately, all Grandmother's moments weren't bad ones.

Lexi woke to the sound of laughter in the kitchen. Hurriedly she dressed and combed her hair. She moved down the stairway listening to the conversation.

"Do you remember the time you and Dad took me fishing, Mom?" Mrs. Leighton was saying.

"Oh, my, yes. Wasn't that a wonderful trip? You fell in the stream so often that I finally let you play in your underwear rather than hang anymore clothes out to dry."

"And I got a sunburn. Do you remember that?"

"And mosquito bites. Your father was upset with me, but you had so much fun. I don't remember, did we catch any fish?"

"Not a one," Marilyn Leighton laughed.

They were reminiscing about old times. Grandmother sounded as clear and normal as she did when they used to visit her in her own home.

"Your wife was quite a fisherwoman back then,

Jim," Grandma said with a chuckle. "Once I found her leaning over the big puddle in our back yard with a long string—a bobby pin tied to the end of it. She said she was fishing for mackerel."

"Did she catch any?" Jim Leighton asked, laughing.

"In fact, she did. There was an old rubber shoe that her father had lost when he was gardening. Got sucked right into the mud. Somehow or another, that little girl pulled out the overshoe with that string and hairpin. Why, that was one of Grandpa's happiest days. Do you remember how we laughed over that overshoe?"

Ben chortled with glee. Lexi entered the kitchen to see her parents sitting at the table. Her grandmother was standing at the stove turning pancakes.

"You're cooking breakfast, Grandma?"

"I hope you're hungry." Grandma peered into the bowl. "I'll have enough pancakes left to feed the United States Army."

"I'm hungry."

"Good girl. You sit right up here. Benjamin, did you eat all that bacon?"

Benjamin giggled and clapped his fork against the plate. "Ben ate it all."

"Well, I'll have to fry a little more then, Lexi," Grandma said.

"No, don't bother. Just give me some of those pancakes."

It felt wonderful to find her family laughing and eating together. It felt so normal. This was like it used to be—before all the trouble started.

"Grandma's been telling us stories about your

mother when she was a little girl, Lexi," Jim Leighton said.

Grandma waved the spatula in the air in Lexi's direction. "And I could tell some tales about you too, my dear. Why, I remember a time when I was babysitting for you, and you got into my closet and tied all the bows on my aprons into knots. You also tied every one of Grandpa's shoelaces together. Why, I was untangling things for weeks after you left!"

Lexi blushed and Ben giggled.

"Poor Grandpa nearly tripped walking out of the bedroom in shoes that still had knots tied in the laces. I think that was the day he decided to wear slip-ons."

The banter continued to be cheerful and playful around the kitchen table. Grandmother put a stack of pancakes on Lexi's plate. "Can you eat more than this?"

Lexi's eyes grew wide. "Grandma, I can't even eat half that many."

Grandma made a disapproving sound. "You're a poor eater."

Lexi took a sip of her orange juice and then began eating her pancakes.

"We should have used bigger glasses, Marilyn," Grandma pointed out. "Lexi's already finished her juice and she's not even half done with the pancakes." Grandma headed for the counter. "Here Lexi, let me pour you some more juice." Before anyone could speak, Grandma reached for the container on the counter and filled Lexi's glass—with maple syrup.

"Oh! Oh my!" Grandma stared at the glass dumbfounded. "Now, why did I do that? Oh, dear. I've made a mess of everything."

The morning's happy mood vanished. Grandma, flustered by her silly mistake, put her hands to her cheeks and began to shake her head. "Oh, why do I do things I don't understand? What's making me so silly and confused? Oh my, oh my."

"It's all right, Mom. It was just a mistake," Mrs. Leighton assured her mother. "It's really no problem."

"It's okay," Ben said. "Lexi likes syrup."

Though the family got past the moment, it was another reminder to Lexi that things still weren't right in their household after all.

———

"Can you come over tonight, Lexi?" Jennifer asked. "Binky's coming. We're going to work on some history."

"Sorry, I can't. I promised I'd be home to help my mother."

"What are you doing over there all the time?" Binky said, her lower lip extending in a pout. "You've been helping her every night after school."

"I promised I'd take my grandmother for a walk. Mother has something special at Ben's school." Lexi wanted to go with her friends. She didn't want to take her grandmother out. Still, Grandmother had been looking forward to going to the store and buying some hairpins and a new bottle of perfume. Lexi felt guilty. How could she say "no" to a perfectly reasonable request?

"Well, if you get a chance, come over later," Jennifer said.

"Thanks. I'll remember that." Lexi walked home alone as she had done so often these past days. It was difficult to talk to any of her friends. She didn't want to tell them about the troubles her family was having. It was easier to be alone.

Mrs. Leighton was waiting for Lexi at the door. "You came just in time. Grandma's all dressed and waiting in the living room for her walk." Mrs. Leighton gave Lexi a kiss on each cheek. "Thanks, honey, I really appreciate this. Grandma's very clear today. You shouldn't have any problems."

"Hello, Lexi," Grandma smiled sweetly as Lexi entered the living room. Her hair was neat and she wore the new pantsuit Lexi's mother had bought for her.

"You look nice today, Grandma."

"Thank you. I'm excited about our walk. It's been such a long time since I've been out of the house." Grandma stood up and moved toward the door, and Lexi followed.

"There's a drugstore about five blocks away. Can you walk that far?"

"Oh, yes. The walk will do me good. I don't want to get fat and lazy, you know," Grandma's eyes twinkled and she patted her nearly concave stomach.

"Well, you're neither of those, Grandma," Lexi assured her. She linked her arm with her grandmother's. Maybe it wasn't going to be such an unpleasant walk after all.

The day was bright and beautiful. Because they were walking slowly to accommodate Grandmother's pace, Lexi had the opportunity to look around and relax.

"The store's just up ahead, Grandma."

"Oh, good. My feet are beginning to tire," Grandma chirped. "Now, what was it I was going to buy?"

Lexi frowned. "Perfume, for one thing."

"Oh, yes. Now I remember," Grandma patted her pocket. "I have a list right here. Is there any other shopping you want to do, Lexi?"

"I could go next door to the hardware store. I need a new chain for my bike."

"That's fine. You just let me do my shopping and come back when you're done with yours."

Lexi stared at her grandmother for a moment, thinking. Should she leave her alone? Grandma seemed so clear and so interested in her surroundings that Lexi decided that it would be all right. "It'll only take me a second to get a bike chain." Lexi escorted her grandmother into the store and introduced her to Mr. Howard, the druggist.

"I'll be right back, Grandma." Hurrying, Lexi went next door and picked out the chain and padlock for her bike.

"Lexi. Hi!" Anna Marie greeted her.

Lexi noticed that Anna was very thin, not at all like the heavy girl she'd been when Lexi first moved to Cedar River.

"Hi there, yourself. What are you up to?"

"Buying a chain for my bike."

"Me too. Did yours get sawed off at school?"

Lexi nodded. "The bike vandals are at it again."

"It's crazy," Anna Marie said, wrinkling her nose. "I don't know what fun they get out of cutting our chains. They don't even steal the bikes!"

"I guess we can be grateful for that," Lexi said with a smile. "I'm getting an extra thick one this time."

The girls visited for a few minutes and Lexi paid for her purchase. When Lexi returned to the drugstore, her grandmother was nowhere in sight. A sick feeling sunk to the pit of her stomach. She hadn't wandered off, had she? Panicky now, Lexi hurried up one aisle and down another.

She was about to burst into tears when she saw Grandmother back in the corner looking at birthday cards.

"Grandma, there you are!" Lexi gasped.

"Oh, yes. Here I am. Look at this card. Isn't it pretty?" Grandma held up one with lilacs and violets. "I love purple flowers, don't you?"

Lexi relaxed enough to smile.

"When is your mother's birthday? I'd like to buy her this card."

Lexi grimaced. "It's next month, Grandma."

"Oh, perfect. Then I'd better get it right now." She took her few purchases to the front counter and paid for them, slowly counting out her money onto the counter as Lexi watched. "One dollar, two dollars, three dollars and here are some quarters."

Lexi could tell that it was a struggle for her grandmother, but she got the right amount and thanked the cashier.

"Just a minute, Grandma. I want to see if the film I brought in last week has been developed yet." Lexi was gone only a few seconds. When she returned, she linked her arm with her grandmother's and they walked from the drugstore into the street. They'd gone about half a block when Grandmother reached into her pocket and pulled out a package of gum.

"Gum, Lexi? Would you like a piece?"

Lexi stared at the gum. Her grandmother *never* chewed gum! She had once told her that gum-chewing was a bad habit—that it made people look like "cows chewing their cud." Lexi had always chewed gum in private whenever Grandma was around.

"Gum? You don't even like gum, Grandma."

"I don't?" Grandma's eyes blinked rapidly.

Lexi felt a knot forming in her throat. "Grandma, where did you get the gum?"

"At the drugstore, of course."

"I didn't see you pay for it."

Grandma's eyes were vague and confused. "Pay for it? It was lying right there by the cash register. I think they wanted me to have it."

Horror washed over Lexi. Her grandmother had shoplifted!

"You're not supposed to do that," Lexi tried to remain calm. "That's stealing, Grandma. You're never supposed to take anything out of a store without paying for it."

Grandmother began to dab at her eyes with a corner of a white lace handkerchief. "It was there. They wanted me to have it. I know they did." She burst into tears.

Much to Lexi's dismay, she felt tears sliding down her own cheeks. They were stopped on the sidewalk, speaking in frantic voices when Mrs. Leighton and Ben pulled up in the car.

"Lexi, what's going on?"

"She was *shoplifting*, Mom," Lexi sobbed.

Mrs. Leighton shook her head. "Get in the car. I'll drive you home."

Grandma, still babbling about the fact that the druggist must have wanted her to have the gum, crawled into the back seat. She looked thin and frail. It only made things seem worse.

Ben's eyes were huge as saucers. No one said another word all the way home.

Mrs. Leighton led her mother into the house and up to her bedroom. She spent half an hour with her getting her to calm down.

When she came downstairs, Mrs. Leighton looked tired and sad. "Lexi, we need to talk."

"I know, Mom. I can't believe Grandma would *shoplift*."

"I understand how you must feel, Lexi. I will go down to the drugstore and talk to them about it and pay for the gum. But right now, I need to talk to you."

"Why did she do it, Mom? That's not anything like Grandma. It's crazy."

"She acted on impulse. In her mind, it seemed right that if the gum was on the counter, within easy reach, it was for her to take."

"But she paid for the other things."

"I know, Lexi, but there's neither rhyme nor reason to this disease."

"I'm so embarrassed I could die." Lexi held her head in her hands. "What if someone had caught her? What would we have done then?"

"You would have had to explain that your grandmother is not well, that she has Alzheimer's disease.

You would have given the gum back or offered to pay for it."

"I would have been so embarrassed!"

"There's no need to be embarrassed, Lexi. You have to think of grandmother the same way that you might think of Ben if he did something wrong. You'd help him through it. You wouldn't scream at him and make him cry."

"Even Ben wouldn't shoplift."

Mrs. Leighton was becoming impatient. "I'm sorry you were embarrassed, Lexi, but you have to understand that your grandmother is not doing these things intentionally." Her mother looked stern. "Now I think you need some quiet time to yourself. Why don't you go up to your room?"

Lexi was hurt and confused. She stamped up the stairs and entered her bedroom, closing the door behind her. She flung herself onto the bed and lay there staring at the ceiling, shivering with anger. She hadn't been sent to her room to calm down since she was a little child!

Everything was out of control. Couldn't her mother see that?

It was all Grandmother's fault—hers and this horrible disease's.

Lexi rolled to her side and gazed at the lamp on her bedside table. Next to it lay her Bible. Lexi groaned and closed her eyes. Seeing it there made her feel worse than ever. She hadn't opened her Bible in over a week.

"I can't, God," she said aloud. "There's nobody in the Bible who's ever had a problem like this one."

Feeling sick and exhausted, Lexi closed her eyes and fell asleep.

Chapter Twelve

"Sing out, people. Sing out." Mrs. Waverly pointed her baton into the air. "Breathe deeply now."

The Emerald Tones were in rehearsal. As usual, Mrs. Waverly was directing with enthusiasm. Her pale blonde hair piled atop her head had started to slip sideways. Three pencils sprouted from her curls.

Lexi felt distanced from the activity around her, as though she were wrapped in plastic, unable to fully hear or see anything that was going on. Though she was present at the practice she could not enjoy it or take part in it.

"Lexi?" Mrs. Waverly called.

Lexi looked up, startled. "Yes?"

"You missed your cue. You have a solo here."

"Oh, I'm sorry," Lexi blushed a deep crimson. "Do you want me to sing now? I won't miss the cue next time." Lexi felt Todd staring at her. She blushed even more.

That strange emotional wrap she was in smothered her senses. The second time through, Lexi managed to sing on cue.

"That's enough for today. Everyone is dismissed." Mrs. Waverly cast Lexi a strange look.

The room emptied quickly. Todd grabbed Lexi by the arm and held her back. "I want to talk to you."

She would have argued, but she'd been avoiding Todd for days. He deserved more than that.

"Let's go into the *River Review* room," he suggested. "It's empty and quiet—a good place to talk."

She followed him to the room where the school paper was done. Lexi wandered aimlessly about, studying the photos she and Todd had taken that were posted on the walls.

"We work well together, don't we," she murmured, admiring a series of basketball photos. Todd had captured a player mid-air. Lexi had gotten a humorous picture of the coach in a huddle, lecturing sternly, his hair standing on end.

"We do make a good team," Todd agreed.

Lexi felt his hand on her arm. "Lexi, stop walking around the room now, like you're trying to avoid talking to me. I need to know why you've been acting so strangely."

Lexi tried to give him an innocent look. "What do you mean by that?"

"Don't pretend you don't know what I'm talking about. Why don't you invite me over to your house anymore? I've always spent a lot of time with Ben and your parents. The past few weeks, I haven't even been allowed inside the front door. What's going on?"

"Oh, it's been so busy, Todd," she waved her hands aimlessly. "I didn't realize it had been that long."

"You know exactly how long it's been."

Lexi dropped her gaze to the floor; her shoulders sagged. "You have to understand, Todd. It's harder to have friends over with my grandmother living there. Things aren't like they used to be. We're always doing something extra for her." Lexi knew her excuses sounded weak and futile.

"Well, it might have to do with your grandmother, but I don't think it's because the house has become too crowded or too busy. Something else is going on." His eyes were pleading. "Lexi, you can talk to me. Tell me what's wrong?"

"Nothing's *wrong*, Todd." Lexi's voice caught in her throat. She turned away to hide the tears forming in her eyes.

"Lexi. Don't do this. You can tell me. What is it about your grandmother? Jennifer and Binky have said the same thing. They haven't been to your house in weeks."

The barriers that Lexi had been struggling so hard to maintain crumbled. Tears flooded her eyes and coursed down her cheeks. "I'm sorry if I've hurt your feelings. I know everyone thinks I'm crazy, but you just can't come over. It would be too awful."

"What would be too awful? Is someone sick?"

"No. Well, yes. Kind of," Lexi looked bewildered.

"Kind of? What do you mean?"

"Oh, Todd!" Lexi flung herself into his arms. "I don't want any of you to see my grandmother the way she is."

"What do you mean?" Todd's voice was gentle with concern. He led her to the old couch in the corner. "Sit down and tell me about this."

"Grandmother *is* sick, Todd. She's sick in her mind. Grandmother has Alzheimer's disease."

"Alzheimer's— I'm not sure I know what that is."

"It affects the brain. It makes my grandmother

act in ways that she's never acted before."

Todd shook his head. "It can't be that bad. What does she do?"

"That's the problem. We never know *what* she's going to do, or what she'll be wearing when she comes downstairs in the morning. Sometimes she looks wonderful. Other times she puts her clothes on backwards. If she walks in front of a mirror, she may begin a conversation with her image. She doesn't even realize she's talking to herself."

"The other morning, she said she was going to pour me some orange juice and she poured me a glassful of maple syrup instead. At night she roams around the house and my parents have to chase after her to make sure she doesn't hurt herself. Mom's taken all the knobs off the stove so Grandma can't turn them on and leave them on. She'll wash clothes all day—without putting any clothes in the washing machine, just soap and water. Todd, I can't tell you how awful it is."

Todd put his arms around Lexi and cradled her gently. "I'm sorry, Lexi. I never realized how bad it was for you at home." He stroked her cheek. "But that's not an excuse to push your friends away. Sounds to me like you need your friends more than ever. Now that I know about your grandmother, if I come to your house, I won't be surprised."

"You can't come to my house," Lexi said. The tears were streaming down her face, but she didn't try to wipe them away. "I'm too ashamed to have anyone see her.

"When Grandpa died, I thought it was the worst thing in the world that could ever happen. Now this.

It's worse than death, Todd. It's like a walking death. Grandma's mind is dying while her body's still well. It's awful. I don't want anyone to see her."

Lexi shuddered. "I took her to the drugstore and she shoplifted! I thought I was going to die. I didn't want to admit to anyone that she was my grandmother."

"That doesn't sound like you," Todd said bluntly. "Lexi, you're one of the most loving, caring persons I've ever known. You're the one who talks about loving people the way they are, about accepting them as God made them. Look at Ben! He's handicapped and you're proud of him." Todd smiled wryly. "I *do* remember that during your first days at Cedar River you tried to keep it a secret, but Ben wouldn't be kept secret for long."

"Those days seem so long ago!"

"Egg is one of our best friends in the whole world," he went on. "He's thin as a rail, scrawny and goofy-looking, but the greatest guy around, don't you agree?"

Lexi couldn't argue with that either.

"And there's Anna Marie," Todd continued, listing others Lexi had insisted on loving just as they were. "She's got an eating problem. First she was too heavy; now she's too thin. You accept her anyway. You tell other people to do the same. Why do you talk that way if you can't accept your own grandmother?"

"This is different, Todd," Lexi protested.

"It *isn't* different, Lexi. You either accept people for what they are, strengths and weaknesses, or you don't. Your grandmother can't help being ill any more than Ben can help being retarded, or Egg can help being skinny, no matter what he does.

"People are the way God made them. Some are prettier than others; some are handsome, some aren't. Some kids are smart or have a nice voice, but it's not because anyone's done something to deserve it. It's a gift from God. You're the one who taught me that, Lexi! Now, after you've convinced me, are you saying that everything you've said wasn't really true?"

Lexi stared at Todd dumbfounded. She'd never thought about it quite like that. The idea gnawed at her insides. "It's just *different*, Todd. Ben's been the way he is since he was a baby. I grew up with Ben's handicap. Besides, he's getting stronger and more fun every day. As for Egg and Anna Marie, they are who they are. Everyone accepts them. But Grandmother *used to be* beautiful and funny and smart. Now she's old and bent and does bizarre things that embarrass me. I *hate* it!"

Todd stared at his friend, his beautiful blue eyes hurt and puzzled. "I don't understand you, Lexi."

"What's to understand? I've tried to explain it to you." Lexi felt a rising sense of panic.

"You're ashamed to let your friends see your grandmother because she might embarrass *you*." Todd repeated evenly.

Lexi nodded. "That's what I said."

"That sounds like a hypocrite to me."

Lexi was shocked. "A hypocrite? You're calling me a hypocrite?"

"If the shoe fits, you'd better wear it," Todd said bluntly.

A hypocrite. Lexi felt as though she'd been slapped in the face.

The Bible said the Pharisees were hypocrites. She remembered the verse that said they were like tombs, white and polished on the outside and filled with dead bones on the inside. Hypocrites were fakes. Imposters. Deceivers. They said one thing and believed another. Hypocrites were double-faced, self-righteous people who said one thing with their lips and believed another in their hearts.

There was nothing Todd could have called her that would have hurt her more.

"How can you say that?" Lexi's eyes flashed and her back grew rigid. "That's a horrible thing to say to me."

"Isn't it true?" Todd looked as upset and angry as Lexi felt. "Why should you tell me or anyone else that we must love others no matter what, when you can't even bring yourself to love your own grandmother when she's sick and needs you so much."

"I *do* love my grandmother. I just don't want to flaunt her in front of everyone so they can laugh at her."

"Can't you trust us? We're your friends, Lexi. Why would we laugh at your grandmother?"

"You couldn't help it. It's so bizarre sometimes. She wets her pants, and she plays in her food. She screams or laughs for no reason at all. You'd laugh, I know you would. You might even tell someone else without thinking, and they'd know how awful it is at my house."

Todd's shoulders sagged. "You don't trust me any-more than that? Not after all the time we've been together?"

"I trust you, Todd," Lexi began. "It's just that I

think this is too tough . . . for you to handle. Every day I feel like I'm living in a keg of dynamite. I don't know when it's going to blow up in my face. Lately Ben's been scared of Grandma because she does such odd things. When I'm around, he hangs on me. My mother and dad are tired because they have to be up at night watching her. She's ruining my life!"

Todd shook his head and said with a hint of sarcasm, "She's ruining *your* life? I think *you* are the one ruining your life, Lexi, not your grandmother. You're choosing not to let your friends into your home. You're choosing to close yourself off with your problem. Maybe your grandmother would *enjoy* seeing some teenagers. Maybe it would make her laugh."

"It would be the other way around," Lexi said bluntly. "She'd make *you* laugh. She'd probably come downstairs wearing a flower pot on her head, or something as strange."

"I've never seen you like this before, Lexi," Todd said, bewildered. "You're just hurt and it's making you angry."

"Shouldn't I be hurt and angry? My boyfriend just called me a hypocrite and accused me of choosing to ruin my own life."

"Think about it, Lexi. I didn't mean it in a hurtful way. It's what I believe is happening."

Lexi couldn't listen. The wound that Todd had caused in her heart was too ragged and painful. "I can't talk about this anymore, Todd. I have to leave." She gathered her books and hurried toward the door.

Todd caught her. "I'm sorry if I've hurt you, Lexi, but I was being honest. Don't push your friends away.

You need them right now. Think about what you're doing. Think about what you're saying. Where's the old Lexi? The Lexi we all know and love?"

"I guess the old Lexi doesn't live here anymore. There's a new one in her place," Lexi said bitterly, "and she doesn't understand what's going on."

She rushed from the room and ran down the hall as fast as she could. When she turned briefly to glance back, Todd was still standing in the classroom door, looking sadly after her.

Chapter Thirteen

The wind whipped through Lexi's hair as she ran toward home, sobbing, choking, gulping back tears. Without speaking to Ben or her grandmother in the living room, Lexi raced up the stairs two at a time and into her bedroom. She slammed the door, locked it, and threw herself onto the bed, crying uncontrollably.

She'd never had a real fight with Todd before. She'd never realized how awful it would be; how empty and aching she might feel inside.

A single word kept echoing through her brain. *Hypocrite. Hypocrite.* That's what Todd thought of her. He thought she had betrayed him and her friends. Was Todd right? She couldn't bear to think that he might have spoken the truth, but the word tormented her. A hypocrite was something that Lexi did not want to be.

She told her mother she wasn't feeling well when she called her for supper. Then she went to bed early and spent a sleepless night, tossing and turning. Every time Lexi dozed off, she could see Todd's face and hear his accusing voice. "Hypocrite, hypocrite, hypocrite." Her brief dreams were filled with slick-tongued people telling her whatever she wanted to hear while all the time she knew they were lying.

At six A.M. Lexi crawled wearily out of bed. She stood in the shower, allowing the hot spray of water to wash across her face. Nothing could wash away her misery.

She dressed quietly and went downstairs before the others were stirring. After grabbing a piece of fruit, she wrote a note to her mother and slipped out of the house. Birds were singing and other early morning sounds were just beginning. It was a quiet, peaceful day. As Lexi walked, she considered her predicament.

Then she realized she was only one block away from the church her family attended. Impulsively, she turned toward the big brick building with its towering spire. She felt compelled to tiptoe up the steps and tug on the front door, expecting it to be locked. To her surprise, it swung open silently. Lexi stepped inside.

She loved this big old church with its beautiful woodwork and peaceful paintings. She particularly liked the picture of Jesus surrounded by wooly lambs gazing up at Him with trusting eyes. He held one baby lamb gently in His arms. The words "I am the Good Shepherd" were written beneath the picture. Lexi closed her eyes, wishing He were there right then to pick her up and to cradle her in His arms. She was still battling the coldness that had grown in her heart ever since her grandfather died.

"Hello. Is someone there?" A voice came from the foyer.

"Hello, Pastor. It's just me, Lexi Leighton."

"Hello, Lexi," the kindly pastor said. "Aren't you out a little early this morning?"

Lexi smiled weakly. "I guess so. I needed to think. I decided to go for a walk and ended up here."

"That happens to me sometimes, too. In fact, last night I had so much on my mind that I couldn't sleep very well. I decided to come over here and work on my sermon for Sunday." He looked at her fondly. "We must both be great thinkers, Lexi." He pushed open the doors to his office. "Would you like to come in?"

Pastor Horace's office was bright and sunny and lined with books. Every shelf and ledge was cluttered with magazines, papers, and memorabilia. There were large photos of his family on the walls and a small one of his wife in a heart-shaped frame on his desk.

"Excuse the mess," he said with a faint smile. "My wife calls me a 'pack rat.' I tell her that I never know when something will become useful for a sermon."

He picked up the papers from the chair by the desk. "Sit down, Lexi. Tell me what you're thinking about so early in the morning." Smile lines creased the corners of his warm blue eyes as he studied Lexi.

This was just what she needed, Lexi thought to herself. Someone kind and understanding—someone not a part of her family. Someone with whom she could share her deepest feelings. "I didn't sleep very well last night," she admitted.

"I can understand why that might happen. I've been visiting with your mother, Lexi. She's told me about your grandmother."

Lexi turned away from the pastor's compassionate gaze. "It's very hard," she admitted.

"I'm sure it is. My own grandfather suffered from something similar. I remember feeling, 'Why me, God? Why us?' It was a great burden for all of us."

"What happened to him?"

Pastor Horace's face was sad. "Oh, eventually he passed away. But not before he taught us a lesson about loving people who can't always return that love in kind." He shook his head slightly. "That was a long time ago, Lexi, and your problems are right here and right now. What can I do to help you?"

"It's not exactly my grandmother that I've been thinking about on this walk," Lexi admitted. "I was wondering, Pastor Horace, what you could tell me about hypocrites."

Pastor Horace looked surprised. "That wasn't the question I expected, Lexi, but it's certainly something I've thought about myself over the years. A hypocrite is someone who pretends to be something better than he or she is. Someone who pretends to be good when he's not, or one who says one thing and does another."

Was that what Todd thought she was? A pretender at goodness? Lexi's heart ached.

Pastor Horace reached for his Bible. "In the book of Matthew, the word 'hypocrite' is mentioned several times. Perhaps the most familiar verse is this one: 'Do not judge, or you too will be judged. For in the same way you judge others, you will be judged, and with the same measure you use, it will be measured to you. Why do you look at the speck of sawdust in your brother's eye and pay no attention to the plank in your own eye? How can you say to your brother,

"Let me take the speck out of your eye," when all the time there is a plank in your own eye? You hypocrite, first take the plank out of your own eye, and then you will see clearly to remove the speck from your brother's eye.' "

"What do you think that means?" Lexi ventured.

"Often it is very easy for us to tell others how to live or tell them what they're doing wrong. Those are the specks in our brothers' eyes. But it's not nearly so easy for us to see the things that *we* are doing wrong. Those are the logs in our own eyes. Until our own hearts and minds are right, we should be careful not to criticize others too harshly."

The pastor warmed to his topic. "In the sixth chapter of Matthew, Scripture warns us to beware of acting pious and religious in public. That's showing off."

He thumbed through the Bible, and began to read aloud: "Be careful not to do your 'acts of righteousness' before men, to be seen by them. If you do, you will have no reward from your Father in heaven. So when you give to the needy, do not announce it with trumpets, as the hypocrites do in the synagogues and on the streets, to be honored by men. I tell you the truth, they have received their reward in full. But when you give to the needy, do not let your left hand know what your right hand is doing, so that your giving may be in secret. Then your Father, who sees what is done in secret, will reward you."

Pastor Horace folded his hands across his Bible and looked thoughtful. "That's a good warning for all of us. Sometimes when we do something kind for someone, or give a particularly big donation to the church, our first impulse is to let others know what we've done.

"The most important thing is our sincere response to God, not doing something to impress others. If your heart is right with God, Lexi, you won't be a hypocrite."

Lexi was silent, and Pastor Horace found one more verse to stress his point. "This is talking about the Pharisees: 'For they do not practice what they preach. They tie up heavy loads and put them on men's shoulders, but they themselves are not willing to lift a finger to move them. Everything they do is done for men to see.' "

Lexi sat slumped in the chair, her mind reeling. Is that what she had done? Had she preached in public what she didn't truly believe or practice in private? Had she wanted others to think she was a Christian, without being right with God in her own heart? Her thoughts made her feel cold and sick.

"Would you like to talk anymore about this, Lexi?" Pastor Horace asked.

Lexi shook her head. "You've given me lots to think about, sir. Thank you very much. If you don't mind, I guess I'd like to be alone for a while."

"When you're ready to talk, Lexi, I'll be here."

Grateful that he hadn't pressed her any further, Lexi excused herself. There was so much to think about. So much to learn.

She left the church and walked slowly toward home, thinking over the past weeks—about her grandfather's death, her grandmother's illness, and the many nights she had gone to sleep without opening her Bible.

It was Todd who had put his finger on the most sore spot of all. It was Todd who made her question whether her outward behavior matched what she believed in her heart.

What *did* she believe about God? How much of what she'd always accepted were beliefs that her parents and grandparents had passed down to her, ideas she'd accepted without thinking? What was the true meaning of Christianity for her?

She'd been taught that God was her Father and that Christ had come to be her Savior. What did that mean to her?

Lexi turned in to the small park three blocks from her home. She found a bench under a spreading oak tree and sat down.

What did she really believe, anyway?

Lexi stared at a little red squirrel, his shiny fur glinting in the sunlight as he scampered across the branches of a big tree.

God had created the squirrel. God had created her. There was no doubt in her mind about that. Surely Anyone who created such masterpieces truly loved His creations!

What's more, God had *shown* His love by sending His Son to die for the people He had created.

Lexi considered her favorite verse in the Bible, John 3:16: "For God so loved the world that he gave his one and only Son, that whoever believes in him, shall not perish, but have eternal life."

She believed with all her heart that the verse was true. God had created her and this beautiful earth. He loved her. He'd sent His Son to die for her. Those weren't ideas she'd accepted without question from her parents. Those were truths she'd seen for herself, her own beliefs, drawn from the experiences of her life!

Lexi's heart lightened. As she sat in the beautiful park, soaking up rays from God's own sun, she felt reassured.

Her faith was *hers*. She could claim it as her own. It was not just family tradition passed down from her parents. Her faith was given to her by God himself.

Deep in her heart, a realization grew. It was her duty to love her grandmother as God had shown His love to her.

Perhaps Todd was right. Perhaps she had behaved like a hypocrite. In the shadow of her grandfather's death and her grandmother's illness, she had doubted God. But the seeds of faith within her were stronger than the seeds of doubt. If she would allow God to nourish those seeds, they would bloom and grow and smother the doubt that had begun to grow in her heart.

The Bible was the place she would go for nourishment to make those seeds of faith strong and healthy.

As she walked toward home, Lexi realized that she hadn't been alone with her thoughts. She had felt the presence of God guiding her, showing her the pathway, encouraging her to take those first hesitant steps. She moved with a lightness in her walk that had been absent for many weeks.

Lexi tipped her head and allowed the warming sun's rays to fall on her face. She sensed she'd been in a battle and she—and God—had finally won.

Lexi was determined that now, with God's help,

she could go home and be more patient and accepting of her grandmother. She would love others as God had loved her. She wasn't perfect, of course, but Lexi knew she could be more patient and caring than she'd been before. God had shown her how.

Lexi's step was determined as she entered the house again. Grandmother was sitting in the living room, holding her shoes in her lap, tying the laces into tiny knots.

"Good morning, Grandma!"

Grandmother didn't look up.

"Lexi," Mrs. Leighton said from the doorway, "Would you please help Grandma get her shoes on? She insists on taking them off and tying the laces in knots. You know she can't go barefoot. She'll stub her toes!"

"Why does she want to keep taking them off, Mom?" Lexi asked.

"The doctor's warned about this, too. Alzheimer's patients fall into patterns of repetition. They do the same things over and over again. I guess we should be happy she's chosen to do something fairly harmless, and not something more dangerous."

Lexi knelt in front of her grandmother and put her hands over the blue veins and wrinkles. "Grandma, this is Lexi. I'm going to help you with your shoes."

Grandmother silently plucked at the laces. Without further comment, Lexi untied the knots and slipped the shoes onto her grandmother's feet. For the first time Lexi could feel the frailty, the confusion and the weakness with understanding.

As she looked on, her grandmother leaned over,

untied the shoes and placed them in her lap again.

Yesterday, Lexi would have felt anger and resentment, even hatred for her grandmother's behavior. Today, she looked at the dear woman with new eyes.

Grandmother was one of God's creatures too. She was old and she was ill, but she was no less precious. With new-found patience, Lexi grasped her grandmother's hands, took the shoes from her lap and put them back on her feet.

So this is what it's like to be a servant, Lexi mused, *to serve others at real cost to yourself.*

Christ had done it.

Lexi had never realized how difficult being a servant could be.

Chapter Fourteen

Perhaps she wasn't cut out to be a servant after all, Lexi thought as impatience welled up in her again. Her grandmother had been particularly irritating lately. It was as though she sensed Lexi's determination to be patient and was testing it to its limits.

While Lexi was at school, her grandmother had come into her room and moved things around, rearranging her desk, the drawers, the closet.

"Mom," Lexi wailed. "She's been in my room again! I can't find anything!"

Lexi held the hairspray bottle she'd found under her pillow and a good silk blouse which had been wadded in the back corner of a drawer.

Marilyn Leighton stepped into the room and put her arm around her daughter. "I'm sorry, honey. I've asked your dad to put a lock on your door. That's the only thing I can think of to stop her from coming in here."

"Then she'll start in your room, or Ben's."

"Then we'll put locks on all the doors, Lexi."

Lexi shook her head grimly. "Look at my mirror."

Mrs. Leighton gasped. Grandmother had scribbled on it with Lexi's lipstick. Even some of Lexi's clothes in the closet had lipstick marks on them. "Oh, honey. I'm *so* sorry."

Lexi choked back a retort. It was just too hard. Grandmother was getting worse every day. The harder Lexi tried to be patient, the more it seemed she was tested. She was feeling strung out and angry again.

"Is that the doorbell?" Mrs. Leighton interrupted her thoughts.

Lexi nodded. "I'll get it. I can't bear to look at this room anymore."

"I'll help you clean it, dear."

Lexi hurried to the stairs, but Todd had already opened the door and stepped inside.

"Todd!"

He had not been to her house since the afternoon of their argument.

"No one answered so I just came inside," Todd said cheerfully. He glanced to the living room where Grandmother sat in the rocker. "Hello, Mrs. Carson," he said politely.

Unexpectedly, Grandmother stopped rocking. Her eyes, usually unfocused and vague, brightened. "There you are! I've been waiting for you. I'm so glad you came."

Grandmother got to her feet and walked toward Todd with scuffing, shuffling steps. Her arms wide open, she embraced him in a hug.

Lexi stared in amazement from the top of the steps.

"My son, my son," Grandma crooned, running her

fingers through Todd's hair. "I thought you'd never get here."

Grandma doesn't have a son.

Todd, rather than pull away, returned the hug and patted her shoulder. "It's very nice to see you, too."

"How have you been? I've been writing to you every day, waiting for you to come," Grandma said.

Todd took her by the hand and led her back to the chair. "That's very nice of you. I'm sure you're a very good letter-writer."

"Oh, yes. Anything for my son." Grandma held his hands and stroked them.

Lexi was moved by the gentleness and compassion with which Todd treated her grandmother. A sharp pang of guilt twisted inside her. His patience was so much greater than her own. Grandmother's behavior wore on everyone's spirits, testing, tugging, trying until their patience was shattered. Even Lexi's parents had begun to be short-tempered with one another.

Lexi walked slowly down the stairs and into the living room.

"My son's here," Grandmother announced with great satisfaction. "See?"

"Yes, I see," Lexi said softly, staring at Todd. "May I take him into the kitchen and offer him something to eat?"

Grandmother nodded. "Yes, I'm sure he's hungry." She patted Todd's head. "You go eat now."

To Lexi's amazement, Todd stood up, leaned over and planted a soft kiss on the top of grandmother's head. He was rewarded with a sweet smile that lifted the old woman's face and made her look beautiful.

"That was awfully nice of you," Lexi admitted once they were in the kitchen.

Todd shrugged. "It was an easy way to make someone happy."

"She doesn't embarrass you or give you the creeps?"

"Maybe a little, but I can stand it. I'm tough." The corner of his mouth formed his wonderful lop-sided grin, and he flexed his muscles. "Remember? I'm Cedar River's top athlete."

Lexi opened the refrigerator and pulled out two colas. "Sometimes I feel like I have to be an athlete to live in this house," she said with a sigh. "Between Grandmother, school, Ben, and the way my parents are wearing out from taking care of Grandma . . ." She shuddered, "I don't want to talk about it."

She quickly changed the subject. "What did you come for?" It felt wonderful to have him there. Lexi wondered how she could have allowed him to stay away so long.

"My mother and I went to the rest home the other day. Several people asked when we were coming back with that good fudge that we make." Todd grinned. "They told me that they missed our visits, but I really think they miss the food."

Lexi clapped her hands to her face. "I'd completely forgotten about that. Were they disappointed?"

"Not really. Just anxious to see us again. Some of those people are very lonely. They aren't as lucky as your grandmother. They don't have a family to care for them."

"Right, lucky," Lexi muttered, but Todd didn't seem to hear.

"We could whip up a couple of batches in just an hour." Todd glanced around the kitchen, but didn't comment on the fact that the stove had no knobs. "We could do it right now."

"Not here."

"Why not?"

Lexi inclined her head toward the living room. "Grandma. She'll just get in the way."

Todd frowned. After a moment of silence, he murmured, "Well, I'm sure my mother will let us use her kitchen."

"It'll be good to get out of the house for a while, too."

Todd didn't understand the pressure of living in this household and there was no way Lexi could explain it to him. Her parents had been going to a support group at the hospital for families who cared for Alzheimer's patients in their homes. They'd learned that no matter how much you loved a person, this illness would make life very difficult.

As they were sitting at the counter and sipping their colas, Grandmother came shuffling into the room. Her eyes darted to and fro as if she were looking for something.

"What is it you want, Grandma?" Lexi asked.

"Lemons," Grandma replied.

"Lemons? What do you want lemons for?"

"To drink."

"Do you want to make lemonade, Grandma?"

"No, no." Grandma looked upset because she could not make Lexi understand. "Oranges."

"You want orange juice?"

Grandma shook her head again. "Not oranges, that other stuff."

"She has a lot of trouble recalling words," Lexi explained to Todd. "Sometimes it's a guessing game that can go on for hours." To her grandmother she said, "You don't want lemons and you don't want oranges, but you're thirsty."

"No color at all," Grandma said.

"What's no color at all?"

Her grandmother stood at the sink and pointed. "That's no color."

"Oh, you want a glass of water!"

Grandmother's shoulders sagged. She sighed with relief. "Yes. Water."

Lexi stepped from the stool and ran water into a plastic tumbler. "Here you go."

Lexi knew Todd was watching her. She could sense his disapproval at her impatient tone.

She'd spent half an hour that morning playing this silly game before Grandma made her understand that they were out of toilet paper in the bathroom.

Lexi was praying for patience. But these days, it seemed, the more patience God gave her, the more she seemed to need.

Lexi took her grandmother by the arm. "Would you like to have a rest?"

Grandma bobbed her white head. "Yes. I'm very sleepy," she said.

"Let me help you up the stairs," Lexi offered. She could feel Todd's gaze. It took several minutes to get

Grandma settled before Lexi could return, and find Todd in the living room.

He was staring out the window toward the street. His hands were tucked neatly into the hip pockets of his jeans. He appeared to be deep in thought. Lexi sensed that Todd was upset, although she couldn't imagine why. She should be the one upset! It was her grandmother causing all the commotion.

Lexi cleared her throat. "I'm back."

Todd spun around on his heels. His handsome face was set, his blue eyes dark. His lips were compressed in a tight line. Lexi had never seen Todd look quite so serious.

"Sorry about that. Took me longer than I expected. Sometimes Grandma takes a while to settle down. She thinks she's got places to go and people to see. Sometimes she thinks that Mom is still a baby and she has to take care of her before she can sleep herself. I know it sounds weird, but I'm almost getting used to it. Dad says we have to 'expect the unexpected' and 'go with the flow.' " Lexi knew she was babbling, but it seemed the only way to hide her discomfort.

It hurt to have Todd see her grandmother so lost and disoriented. Lexi had been much more impatient with her than she'd intended to be.

Ever since that day in the park, her attitude had been dramatically changed toward her grandmother. She'd learned to rejoice over Grandma's good days. When things were at their worst, Lexi reminded herself that her grandmother was precious in God's eyes.

Lexi had returned to her Bible and could genuinely feel God working within her. The iciness that had surrounded her heart in the days since Grand-father's death was slowly thawing. The personal realization of what God meant to her had given her strength.

Todd couldn't realize how much she'd struggled or how far she'd come in these past days.

She still had a long way to go, however, Lexi mused. Accepting Grandmother for what she'd become was one thing—allowing her personal friends to see her grandmother and have them make their own judgments was quite another.

"Is something wrong, Todd?" she asked. "You look upset."

His voice was accusing. "You've changed, Lexi."

Lexi couldn't deny that. She *had* changed—several times, in fact, in the past weeks. She'd changed from a happy person to an angry and resentful one. Now, in the last few days, she'd found some control again. Even more, she had a growing sense of peace within her.

"Maybe I have changed, Todd," Lexi admitted. "But why are you upset with me?"

"Can't you see what you're doing to your grand-mother?" he blurted. His hands came out of his pockets. "She can't help the way she is! You rush her along like she were a little child."

"She is a little child, Todd," Lexi attempted to explain patiently. "In her mind, that's what she is. Sometimes she can't remember words or whether or not she's eaten or gone to the bathroom. She *is* like a little child."

"I think you're too impatient with her, Lexi. You seemed almost unkind."

Unkind. The word hurt Lexi. When she'd come so far in learning to be patient and loving with Grandmother, Todd was accusing her of being unkind?

The injustice of it all washed over Lexi. "You're not being fair, Todd."

"What's fair about the way you hustle her off to bed in the middle of the day just because she's embarrassing you?" Todd retorted indignantly.

Lexi knew how tender Todd was and how distressing it must be to see anyone like her grandmother. But two words rang out in her mind. *Hypocrite* and *unfair*.

Twice he'd hurt her. Didn't he understand what his words could do?

"You don't understand, Todd," Lexi protested. "It might seem to you that I'm being unkind to Grandmother, but I'm not at all. We do love her."

"But it's not right," Todd said with anguish in his voice. "She's a person too. She shouldn't be hidden away upstairs just because I'm here."

"I didn't do that!" The strands of Lexi's temper were fraying rapidly. "How dare you criticize what I do for my grandmother? You haven't been here in weeks! You don't know how it's been for us."

"You've never invited me," he shot back.

"I guess now I know the reason why," Lexi said indignantly. Her heart was breaking. She and Todd had never argued like this. Their words were terse and hard. The look in Todd's eyes was almost unbearable.

He ran his long fingers through his hair. "I just don't get it Lexi. I don't understand."

"And you think I do? I can't understand why this whole disease happens to anyone." Lexi realized her voice was rising. "I hate it, Todd. I hate this disease with all my heart and with all my mind, but it doesn't mean I don't love my grandmother. I've learned to accept her as she is. You'll have to do that too."

It was suddenly clear to Lexi what was happening. Gentle, kindhearted Todd was confused and angered to see what her grandmother had become. Frustrated, he'd turned that anger on Lexi.

Lexi extended a hand to show him that she understood, that she'd been through the same struggle.

He shook his head and took a step backward. "I don't want to talk about this right now. You and I aren't on the same wave length." He backed toward the door.

"Todd. I know what you're feeling. Let me try to help you."

"I don't know you anymore, Lexi," he muttered, confusion in his voice. Suddenly, he spun around and grabbed the doorknob. "I've got to go, Lexi. Goodbye."

He left her standing in the doorway. It was so unlike him. Todd was gone. A new emptiness welled up within Lexi's heart.

So this is what it's like to have a broken heart, she thought.

She clutched at her chest willing away the pain that lodged there. He was gone. He might never come back.

"Now what, God?" Tears streamed down Lexi's face. "I've lost everything, haven't I? First my grandfather, then my grandmother, and now Todd!"

But you haven't lost Me.

Lexi blinked. The thought came to her so clearly that it was as if it had been spoken out loud.

But you haven't lost Me.

Lexi sank to the couch. She hadn't lost God. He was there, in her mind and heart, reminding her that He had not gone away.

A spark of hope flickered.

God was still with her as He had promised He would be. He would be her strength. He would help mend her broken heart.

Lexi's mother found her nearly an hour later, curled into a ball on the sofa, her face buried in a pillow.

"Lexi, is everything all right?"

"Not really."

"Did Todd leave? You look as though you've lost your best friend."

Lexi gave a weak smile. She nodded. "I've lost a lot of my friends lately, Mom. Fortunately, my Very Best Friend in the whole world is still with me."

Mrs. Leighton patted Lexi's arm. She understood. "He's my Best Friend, too, Lexi. As long as we have Him on our side, weeping with us, rejoicing with us, things are going to be all right."

Lexi sighed. She sincerely hoped her Best Friend could help her with her problems. There was no way she could solve them on her own.

———

Will Lexi's faith in God carry her through the trials ahead? Is Todd gone from her life forever? Find the answers in Cedar River Daydreams Book #10, *Tomorrow's Promise*.

A Note From Judy

I'm glad you're reading *Cedar River Daydreams*! I hope I've given you something to think about as well as a story to entertain you. If you feel you have any of the problems that Lexi and her friends experience, I encourage you to talk with your parents, a pastor, or a trusted adult friend. There are many people who care about you!

Also, I enjoy hearing from my readers, so if you'd like to write, my address is:

Judy Baer
Bethany House Publishers
6820 Auto Club Road
Minneapolis, MN 55438

Please include an addressed, stamped envelope if you would like an answer. Thanks.